THE CAMPFIRE GIRLS
SERIES

❧

A CAMPFIRE GIRL'S FIRST COUNCIL FIRE

A CAMPFIRE GIRL'S CHUM

A CAMPFIRE GIRL IN SUMMER CAMP

A CAMPFIRE GIRL'S ADVENTURE

A CAMPFIRE GIRL'S TEST OF FRIENDSHIP

A CAMPFIRE GIRL'S HAPPINESS

Dolly was bound to a tree, a handkerchief over her mouth.

A Campfire Girl in Summer Camp

By
JANE L. STEWART

CAMPFIRE GIRLS SERIES
VOLUME III

WILDSIDE PRESS

The Camp Fire Girls at Long Lake

CHAPTER I

A GROUNDLESS JEALOUSY

"I told you we were going to be happy here, didn't I, Zara?"

The speaker was Dolly Ransom, a black-haired, mischievous Wood Gatherer of the Camp Fire Girls, and a member of the Manasquan Camp Fire, the Guardian of which was Miss Eleanor Mercer, or Wanaka, as she was known in the ceremonial camp fires that were held each month. The girls were staying with her at her father's farm, and only a few days before Zara, who had enemies determined to keep her from her friends of the Camp Fire, had been restored to them, through the shrewd suspicions that a faithless friend had aroused in Bessie King, Zara's best chum.

Zara and Dolly were on top of a big wagon, half filled with new-mown hay, the sweet smell of which delighted Dolly, although Zara, who had lived in the country, knew it too well to become wildly enthusiastic over anything that was so commonplace to her. Below them, on the ground, two other Camp Fire Girls in the regular working costume of the Camp Fire—middy blouses and wide blue bloomers—were tossing up the hay, under the amused direction of Walter Stubbs, one of the boys who worked on the farm.

"I'm awfully glad to be here with the girls again, Dolly," said Zara. "No, that's not the way! Here, use your rake like this. The way you're doing it the wagon won't hold half as much hay as it should."

"Is Bessie acting as if she was your teacher, Margery?" Dolly called down laughingly to Margery Burton, who, because she was always laughing, was called Minnehaha by the Camp Fire Girls. "Zara acts just as if we were in school, and she's as superior and tiresome as she can be."

"She's a regular farm girl, that Zara," said Walt, with a grin. "Knows as much about packin' hay as I do—'most. Bessie, thought you'd lived on a farm all yer life. Zara there can beat yer all hollow at this. You're only gettin' half a pickful every time you toss the hay up. Here—let me show you!"

"I'd be a pretty good teacher if I tried to show Margery, Dolly," laughed Bessie King. "You hear how Walter is scolding me!"

"He's quite right, too," said Dolly, with a little pout. "You know too much, Bessie—I'm glad to find there's something you don't do right. You must be stupid about some things, just like the rest of us, if you lived on a farm and don't know how to pitch hay properly after all these years!"

Bessie laughed. Dolly's smile was ample proof that there was nothing ill-natured about her little gibe.

"Girls on farms in this country don't work in the fields—the men wouldn't let them," said Bessie. "They'd rather have them stay in a hot kitchen all day, cooking and washing dishes. And when they want a change, the men let them chop wood, and fetch water, and run around to collect the eggs, and milk the cows, and churn butter and fix the garden truck! Oh, it's easy for girls and women on a farm—all they have to do is a few little things like that. The men do all the hard work. You wouldn't let your wife do more than that, would you, Walter?"

The boy flushed.

"When I get married, I'm aimin' to have a hired gal to do all them chores," he said. "They's some farmers seem to think when they marry they're just gettin' an extra lot of hired help they don't have to pay fer, but we don't figger that way in these parts. No, ma'am."

He looked shyly at Dolly as he spoke, and Dolly, who was an accomplished little flirt, saw the look and understood it very well. She tossed her pretty head.

"You needn't look at me that way, Walt Stubbs," she said. "I'm never going to marry any farmer—so there! I'm going to marry a rich man, and live in the city, and have my own automobile and all the servants I want, and never do anything at all unless I like. So you needn't waste your breath telling me what a good time your wife is going to have."

Walter, already as brown as a berry from the hot sun under which he worked every day, turned redder than he had been before, if that was possible. But, wisely, he made no attempt to answer Dolly. He had already been inveigled into two or three arguments with the sharp witted girl from the city, and he had no mind for any more of the cutting sarcasm with which she had withered him up each time just as he thought he had got the best of her.

Still, in spite of her sharp tongue and her fondness for teasing him, Walt liked Dolly better than any of the girls from the city who were staying on the farm, and he was always glad to welcome her when she appeared where he was working, even though she interrupted his work, and made it necessary for him to stick to his job after the others were through in order to make up for lost time. But Dolly had little use for him, in spite of his obvious devotion, which all the other girls had noticed. And this time his silence didn't save him from another sharp thrust.

"Goin' to that ice-cream festival over to the Methodist Church at Deer Crossin' to-night?" she asked him, trying to imitate his peculiar country accent.

"I'm aimin' to," he said uncomfortably. "You said you was goin' to let me take you. Isn't that so?"

"Oh, yes—I suppose so," she said, tossing her head again. "But I never said I'd let you bring me home, did I? Maybe I'll find some one over there I like better to come home with."

Walter didn't answer, which proved that, young as he was, and inexperienced in the ways of city girls like Dolly, he was learning fast. But just then a bell sounded from the farm, and the girls dropped their pitchforks quickly.

"Dinner time!" cried Margery Burton, happily. "Come on down, you two, and we'll go over to that big tree and eat our dinner in the shade. Walter, if you'll go and fetch us a pail of water from the spring, we'll have dinner ready when you get back. And I bet you'll be surprised when you see what we've got, too— something awfully good. We got Mrs. Farnham to let us put up the best lunch you ever saw!"

"Yes you did!" gibed Walter. He wasn't half as much afraid of Margery and the other girls, who never teased him, as he was of Dolly Ransom, and he didn't like them as well, either. Perhaps it was just because Dolly made a point of teasing him that he was so fond of her. But

he picked up the pail, obediently enough, and
went off. When he was out of hearing Bessie
shook her finger reproachfully at Dolly.

"I thought you were going to be good and
not tease Walter any more!" she said, half
smiling.

'Oh, he's so stupid—it's just fun to tease
him, and he's so easy that I just can't help it,"
said Dolly.

"I don't think he's stupid—I think he's a very
nice boy," said Bessie. "Don't you, Margery?"

"I certainly do, Bessie—much too nice for a
little flirt like Dolly to torment him the way she
does."

"Well, if you two like him so much you can
have him, and welcome!" cried Dolly, tossing
her head. "I'm sure I don't want him tag-
ging around after me all the time the way he
does."

"Better be careful, Dolly," advised Margery,
who knew her of old. "They say pride goes
before a fall, and if you're not nice to him you

may have to come home from the festival to-
night without a beau—and you know you wouldn't
like that."

"I'd just as soon not have a beau at all as
have some of these boys around here," declared
Dolly, pugnaciously. "I like the country, but I
don't see why the people have to be so stupid.
They're not half as bright as the ones we know
in the city."

"I don't know about that, Dolly. Bessie's
from the country, but I think she's as bright as
most of the people in the city. They haven't
been able to fool her very much since she left
Hedgeville, you know."

"Oh, I didn't mean Bessie!" cried Dolly,
throwing her arms around Bessie's neck affec-
tionately. "You know I didn't, don't you, dear?
And I'm only joking about half the time anyhow, when I say things like that."

"Here comes Walter now—we'll see whether
he doesn't admit that this is the best dinner he
ever ate in the fields!" said Margery.

It was, too. There was no doubt at all about
that. There were cold chicken, and rolls, and
plenty of fresh butter, and new milk, and hard
boiled eggs, that the girls had stuffed, and a luscious blueberry pie that Bessie herself had been
allowed to bake in the big farm kitchen. They
made a great dinner of it, and Walter was loud
in his praises.

"That certainly beats what we have out here
most days!" he said. "We have plenty—but it's
just bread and cold meat and water, as a rule,
and no dessert. It's better than they get at
most farms, though, at that."

When the meal was finished the girls quickly
made neat parcels of the dishes that were to be
taken back, and all the litter that remained under
the tree was gathered up into a neat heap and
burned.

"My, but you're neat!" exclaimed Walter, as
he watched them.

"It's one of our Camp Fire rules," explained
Margery. "We're used to camping out and eat-

ing in the open air, you know, and it isn't fair
to leave a place so that the next people who
camp out there have to do a lot of work to clean
up after you before they can begin having a
good time themselves. We wouldn't like it if we
had to do it after others, so we try always to
leave things just as we'd like to find them ourselves. And it wouldn't be good for the Camp
Fire Girls if people thought we were careless and
untidy.''

Then they got back to work again, and the long
summer afternoon passed happily, with all four
of the girls doing their share of the work. The
sun was still high when they had finished their
work, and Walter gave the word to stop happily,
since he wanted time to put on his best clothes
for the trip to Deer Crossing, where the ice-
cream festival was to be held. Such festivities
were rare enough in the country to be made
mightily welcome when they came, especially
when the date chosen was a Saturday, since on
Sunday those who worked in the fields every

other day of the week could take things easily and lie abed late.

"Well, I'll see all you girls again to-night," he said. "I'll be along after supper, Dolly— don't forget. We're goin' to ride over together in the first wagon."

"All right," said Dolly, smiling at him, and winking shamelessly at Bessie. "Don't forget to put on that new blue necktie and to wear those pink socks, Walter."

"I sure won't," he said, not having seen her wink, and, as he turned away, Dolly looked at Bessie with a gesture of comic despair.

"I think it's very mean to laugh at Walter's clothes, Dolly," said Bessie. "They're not a bit sillier than some of the things the boys in the city wear, are they, Margery?"

"I should say not—not half as foolish. I've seen some of your pet boys wearing the sort of clothes one would expect men at the racetrack to wear, and nobody else, Dolly. You want to get over thinking you're so much better than everyone else—if you don't, it's going to make you unhappy.''

Once they were at the ice-cream festival, where all the girls and young fellows from miles around seemed to have gathered, Dolly seemed prepared to have a very good time, however. She entered into the spirit of the occasion, and, though she, like Bessie and most of the Camp Fire Girls, would not take part in the kissing games that were popular, she wasn't a bit stiff or superior.

''I wonder where that nice boy that thrashed Jake Hoover is?'' she asked Bessie, after they had been there for a while.

''Oh, that's whom you're looking for!'' exclaimed Bessie, with a laugh. ''Will Burns, you mean? That's so, Dolly—he said he was coming here, didn't he?''

''He certainly did. I'd like to see him again, Bessie. He wasn't as stupid as most of these country boys.''

''He was splendid,'' said Bessie, warmly. ''If it hadn't been for him, I might not be here now,

Dolly. Jake would have got me back into the other state—he was strong enough to make me go where he wanted. And if I'd been caught there, they'd have made me stay."

"There he is now!" exclaimed Dolly, as a tall, sunburned boy appeared in the doorway. "I was beginning to be afraid he wasn't coming at all."

Will Burns, who was a cousin of Walter Stubbs, seemed to be well known to the young people of the neighborhood, though his home was near Jericho, some twenty miles away. He was greeted on all sides as he made his way through the Sunday School room, where the festival was being held, and it was some minutes before the girls from the farm saw that he was nearing them.

"Well—well, so you got home all right?" he said, smiling at Bessie. "I thought you wouldn't have any more trouble, once you got on the train. I'm glad to see you again."

And then Dolly's vanity got a rude shock.

For Will Burns began to devote himself at once, after he had greeted Dolly and been introduced to Zara and some of the other girls, to Bessie. Everyone in the room soon noticed this, and since most of the girls there had tried to make him pay attention to them, at one time or another, his evident fondness for Bessie caused a little sensation. Dolly, so surprised to find a boy she fancied willing to talk to anyone else that she didn't know what to do, stood it as long as she could, and then went in search of Walter Stubbs, whom she had snubbed unmercifully all evening.

But Walter had at last plucked up courage enough to resent the way she treated him, and she found that he had bought two plates of ice-cream for Margery Burton and himself, and that they were sitting in a corner, eating their ice-cream, and talking away as merrily as if they had known one another all their lives!

Eleanor Mercer, who had come over to have an eye on the girls, saw the little comedy. She was sorry for Dolly, who was sensitive, but she knew that the lesson would be a wholesome one for the little flirt, who had been flattered so much by the boys in the city that she had come to believe that she could make any boy do just what she desired. So she said nothing, even when Dolly, without a single boy to keep her in countenance, was reduced to sitting with one or two other girls who were in the same predicament, since there were more girls there than boys.

Walter did not even come to get her to ride home with him. Instead, he found a place with Margery Burton, and Dolly had to climb into her wagon alone. There she found Bessie.

"You're a mean old thing, Bessie King!" she said, half crying.

CHAPTER II

Dolly had spoken in a low tone, her sobs seeming to strangle her speech, and only Bessie, who was amazed by this outburst, heard her. Grieved and astonished, she put her arm about Dolly, but the other girl threw it off, roughly.

"Don't you pretend you love me—I know the mean sort of a cat you are now!" she said bitterly.

"Why, Dolly! Whatever *is* the matter with you? What have I done to make you angry?"

"If you were so mad at me the other day for getting you into that automobile ride with Mr. Holmes you might have said so—instead of pretending that you'd forgiven me, and then turning around and making everyone laugh at me tonight! You're prettier than I am—and clever—

27

but I think it's pretty mean to make that Burns
boy spend the whole evening with you!''

Gradually, and very faintly, Bessie began to
have a glimmering of what was wrong with her
friend. She found it hard work not to smile, or
even to laugh outright, but she resisted the temp-
tation nobly, for she knew only too well that to
Dolly, sensitive and nervous, laughter would be
just the one thing needed to make it harder than
ever to patch up this senseless and silly quarrel,
which, so far, was only one sided.

To Bessie, who thought little of boys, and to
whom jealousy was alien, the idea that Dolly was
really jealous of her seemed absurd, since she
knew how little cause there was for such a feel-
ing. But, very wisely, she determined to proceed
slowly, and not to do anything that could possibly
give Dolly any fresh cause of offence.

''Dolly,'' she said, ''you mustn't feel that
way. Really, dear, I didn't do that at all. I
talked to him when he came to sit down by me,
but that was all. I couldn't very well tell him to

go away, or not answer him when he spoke to me, could I?''

''Oh, I know what you're going to say—that it was all his fault. But if you hadn't tried to make him come he wouldn't have done it.''

''I didn't try to make him come. Did you?''

Dolly stared at her a moment. The question seemed to force her to give attention to a new idea, to something she had not thought of before. But when she spoke her voice was still defiant.

''Suppose I did!'' she said angrily. ''I wanted to have a good time—and he was the nicest boy there—''

''Maybe he saw that you were waiting for him too plainly, Dolly. Maybe he wanted to pick out someone for himself—and if you'd pretended that you didn't care whether he talked to you or not he would have been more anxious to be with you.''

Dolly blushed slightly at that, though it was too dark for Bessie to see the color in her cheeks. She knew very well that Bessie was right, but she wondered how Bessie knew it. That feigned

indifference had brought her the attentions of
more than one boy who had boasted that he was
not going to pay any attention to her just because everyone else did.

But the gradually dawning suspicion that she
might, after all, have only herself to blame for
the spoiling of her evening's fun, and that she
had acted in rather a silly fashion, didn't soften
Dolly particularly. Very few people are able
to recover a lost temper just because they find
out, at the height of their anger, that they are
themselves to blame for what made them angry,
and Dolly was not yet one of them.

"I suppose you'll tell all the other girls about
this," she said. She wasn't crying any more,
but her voice was as hard as ever. "I think
you're horrid—and I thought I was going to
like you so much. I think I'll ask Miss Eleanor
to let me share a room with someone else."

Bessie didn't answer, though Dolly waited while
the wagon drove on for quite a hundred yards.
Bessie was thinking hard. She liked Dolly; she

was sure that this was only a show of Dolly's temper, which, despite the restrictions that surrounded her in her home, and had a good deal to do with her mischievous ways, had never been properly curbed.

But, though Bessie was not angry in her turn, she understood thoroughly that if she and Dolly were to continue the friendship that had begun so promisingly, this trouble between them must be settled, and settled in the proper fashion. If Dolly were allowed to sleep on her anger, it would be infinitely harder to restore their relations to a friendly basis.

"I suppose you don't care!" said Dolly, finally, when she decided that Bessie was not going to answer her.

And now Bessie decided on a change of tactics. She had tried arguing with Dolly, and it had seemed to do no good at all. It was time to see if a little ridicule would not be more useful.

"I didn't say so, Dolly," she answered, very quietly. And she smiled at her friend. "What's the use of my saying anything? I told you the truth about what happened this evening, and you didn't believe me. So there's not much use talking, is there?''

''You know I'm right, or you'd have plenty to talk about,'' said Dolly, unhappily. ''Oh, I wish we'd never seen Will Burns!''

''I wish we hadn't seen him until to-night, Dolly,'' said Bessie, gravely. ''You know, that trip in the automobile with Mr. Holmes the other day wasn't very nice for me, Dolly. If they had caught me, as Mr. Holmes had planned to do, I'd have been taken back to Hedgeville, and bound over to Farmer Weeks—and he's a miser, who hates me, and would have been as mean to me as he could possibly be. That's how we met Will Burns, you know—because you insisted on going with Mr. Holmes in his car to get an ice-cream soda.''

''That's just what I said—you pretended to forgive me for that, and you haven't at all— you're still angry, and you humiliated me before

all those people just to get even! I didn't think
you were like that, Bessie—I thought you were
nicer than I. But—"

"Dolly, stop talking a little, and just think it
over. You say you didn't have a good time, and
you mean that you didn't have a boy waiting
around to do what you told him all evening.
Isn't that so?"

"All the other girls had boys around them all
the time—"

"You went with Walter Stubbs, didn't you?
And you told him that maybe you'd come home
with him and maybe you wouldn't—and that if
anyone you liked better came along you were
going to stay with them. You didn't know Will
Burns was coming, did you?"

"No, but—I thought if he did come—"

"That's just it. You didn't think about Walter
at all, did you. You wanted to have a good time
yourself—and you didn't care what sort of a
time he had? You just thought that if Will
Burns did come he was sure to want to be with

you, and so, as soon as you saw him come in you
sent Walter off. Oh, you were silly, Dolly—and
it was all your own fault. Don't you think it's
rather mean to blame me? We were together
when Will Burns was coming toward us, and I
wanted to go away and let you stay there—but
you said I must stay. Don't you remember that?''

Dolly, as a matter of fact, had quite forgotten
it. But she remembered well enough, now that
Bessie had reminded her of it. And, though she
had a hot temper, and was fond of mischief,
Dolly was not sly. She admitted it at once.

"I do remember it now, Bessie."

"Well, don't you see how absurd it is to say
that I took Will away from you? We were both
there together—I couldn't tell when we saw him
coming that he was going to talk to me, could
I? And listen, Dolly—he asked me to go home
with him in his buggy, and I said I wouldn't.''

With some girls that would have made the
chance of mending things very remote. But
Dolly, although her jealousy had been so quickly

aroused, was not the sort to get still angrier at this fresh proof that she had been mistaken in thinking that Will Burns had liked her better than Bessie.

"Why, Bessie—why did you do that?"

Bessie laughed.

"We're not going to be here very much longer, are we, Dolly?" she said. "Well—if we're not going to be here, we're not going to see much of Will Burns. You're not the only girl who— was—who thought that he ought to be paying more attention to her than to me. There was a pretty girl from Jericho, and he's known her a long time. Walter told me about them.

"And I could see that she wanted him to drive her home, so I asked him why he didn't do it. And he got very much confused, but he went over to her, finally, and she looked just as happy as she could be when he handed her up into his buggy, and they all went off along the road together, Will and she and two or three other fellows who had driven over together from Jericho."

Dolly's expression had changed two or three times, very swiftly, as she listened. Now she sighed, and her hand crept out to find Bessie's.

"Oh, Bessie," she said, softly, "won't you forgive me, dear? I've made a fool of myself again —I'm always doing that, it seems to me. And every time I promise myself or you or someone not to do it again. But the trouble is there are so many different ways of being foolish. I seem to find new ones all the time, and every one is so different from the others that I never know about it until it's too late."

"It's never too late to find out one's been in the wrong, Dolly, if one admits it. There aren't many girls like you, who are ready to say they've been wrong, no matter how well they know it. I haven't anything to forgive you for—so don't let's talk any more about that. Everyone makes mistakes. If I thought anyone had treated me as you thought I had treated you to-night I'd have been angry, too."

Poor Dolly sighed disconsolately.

"You're the best friend I ever had, Bessie,"
she said. "I make everyone angry with me, and
when I say I'm sorry, they pretend that they've
forgiven me, but they haven't, really, at all.
That's why I said that about your still being
angry with me. I thought you must be. I really
am going to try to be more sensible."

And so the little misunderstanding, which might
easily, had Bessie been less patient and tactful,
have grown into a quarrel that would have ended
their friendship before it was well begun, was
smoothed over, and Dolly and Bessie, tired but
happy, went upstairs to their room together, and
were asleep so quickly that they didn't even take
the time to talk matters over.

Eleanor Mercer, standing in the big hall of
the farm house as the girls went upstairs, smiled
after Dolly and Bessie.

"I think you thought I was foolish to put
those two in a room together," she said to Mrs.
Farnham, the motherly housekeeper, whom Eleanor had known since, as a little girl, she had
played about the farm.

"I wouldn't say that, Miss Eleanor," said Mrs. Farnham. "I didn't see how they were going to get along together, because they were so different. But it's not for me to say that you're foolish, no matter what you do."

"Oh, yes, it is," laughed Eleanor. "You used to have to tell me I was foolish in the old days, when I wanted to eat green apples, and all sorts of other things that would have made me sick, and just because I'm grown up doesn't keep me from wanting to do lots of things that are just as foolish now. But I do think I was right in that."

"They do seem to get on well," agreed Mrs. Farnham.

"It's just because they are so different," said Eleanor. "Dolly does everything on impulse— she doesn't stop to think. With Bessie it's just the opposite. She's almost too old—she isn't impulsive enough. And I think each of them will work a little on the other, so that they'll both benefit by being together. Bessie likes looking after people, and she may make Dolly think a little more.

"There isn't a nicer, sweeter girl in the whole Camp Fire than Dolly, but lots of people don't like her, because they don't understand her. Oh, I'm sure it's going to be splendid for both of them. Dolly was awfully angry at Bessie before they started from the church—but you saw how they were when they got here to-night?"

"I did, indeed, Miss Eleanor. And I'd say Dolly has a high temper, too, just to look at her."

"Oh, she has—and Bessie never seems to get angry. I don't understand that—it's my worst fault, I think. Losing my temper, I mean. Though I'm better than I used to be. Well—good-night."

The next day was Sunday, and, of course, there was none of the work about the farm that the girls of the Camp Fire enjoyed so much. They went to church in the morning, and when they returned Bessie was surprised to see Charlie Jamieson, the lawyer, Eleanor Mercer's cousin,

sitting on the front piazza. Eleanor took Bessie
with her when she went to greet him.

"No bad news, Charlie?" she said, anxiously.
He was looking after the interests of Bessie and
of Zara, whose father, unjustly accused as Charlie
and the girls believed, of counterfeiting, was in
prison in the city from which the Camp Fire
Girls came. Charlie Jamieson had about decided
that his imprisonment was the result of a con-
spiracy in which Farmer Weeks, from Bessie's
home town, Hedgeville, was mixed up with a Mr.
Holmes, a rich merchant of the city. The reason
for the persecution of the two girls and of Zara's
father was a mystery, but Jamieson had made
up his mind to solve it.

"No—not bad news, exactly," he said. "But
I've had a talk with Holmes, and I'm worried,
Eleanor. You know, that was a pretty bold thing
he did the other day, when he trapped Bessie
into going with him for an automobile ride and
tried to kidnap her. That's a serious offense,
and a man in Holmes's position in the city

wouldn't be mixed up in it unless there was a very important reason. And from the way he talked to me I'm more convinced than ever that he will just be waiting for a chance to try it again.''

''What did he say to you, Charlie?''

''Oh, nothing very definite. He advised me to drop this case. He reminded me that he had a good deal of influence—and that he could bring me a lot of business, or keep it away. And he said that if I didn't quit meddling with this business I'd have reason to feel sorry.''

''What did you tell him?''

''To get out of my office before I kicked him out! He didn't like that, I can tell you. But I noticed that he got out. But here's the point. Are you still planning that camping trip to Long Lake?''

''Yes—I think it would be splendid there.''

''Well, why don't you start pretty soon? Holmes knows this country very well, and he's got so much money that, if he spends it, he can

probably find people to do what he wants. Up
there it's lonely country, and pretty wild, and you
could keep an eye on Bessie and Zara even better
than you can here. I don't know why he wants
to have them in his power, but it's quite evident
that their plans depend on that for success, and
our best plan, as long as we're in the dark this
way, and don't know the answer to all these
puzzling things, is to keep things as they are.
I'm convinced that they can't do anything that
need worry us much as long as we have Bessie
and Zara safe and sound.''

''We can start to-morrow,'' said Eleanor.
''Bessie—will you tell the girls to get ready?
I'll go and make arrangements, Charlie.''

And so, the next day, after lunch, the Camp
Fire Girls, waving their hands to kindly Mrs.
Farnham, and making a great fuss over Walter,
who drove them to the station, said good-bye
for the time, at least, to the farm. And Dolly
Ransom, Bessie noticed, took pains to be particularly nice to Walter Stubbs.

CHAPTER III

LONG LAKE

"I love traveling," said Dolly, when they were settled in their places in the train that was to take them up into the hills and on the first stage of the journey to Long Lake. "I like to see new places and new people."

"Dolly's never content for very long in one place," said Eleanor Mercer, who overheard her remark, smiling. "If she had her way she'd be flying all over the country all the time. Wouldn't you, Dolly?"

"I don't like to know what's going to happen next all the time," said Dolly.

"I know just how you feel," Bessie surprised her by saying. "I used to think, sometimes, when I was on Paw Hoover's farm in Hedgeville, that if only I could go to sleep some night without knowing just what was going to happen the next

43

day I'd be happy. It was always the same, too—
just the same things to do, and the same places
to see—"

"I should think Jake Hoover would have kept
you guessing what he was going to do next,"
said Dolly, spitefully. "The great big bully! Oh,
how glad I was when Will Burns knocked him
down the other day!"

"Yes," admitted Bessie. "I didn't know just
what Jake was going to tell Maw Hoover about
me next—but then, you see, I always knew it was
something that would get me into trouble, and
that I'd either get beaten or get a scolding and
have to do without my supper. So even about
that it wasn't very difficult to know what was
going to happen."

"Heavens—I'd have run away long before you
did," said Dolly, with a shudder. "I don't see
how you ever stood it as long as you did, Bessie.
It must have been awful."

"It was, Dolly," said Eleanor, gravely. "I was
there, and I made a point of looking into things,

so that if anyone ever blamed me for helping Bessie and Zara to get away, I could explain that I hadn't just taken Bessie's word for things. But running away was a pretty hard thing to do. It's easy to talk about—but where was Bessie to go? She isn't like you—or she wasn't.

"She didn't have a lot of friends, who would have thought it was just a fine joke for her to have to run off that way. If you did it, you'd have a good time, and when you got tired of it, you'd go back to your Aunt Mabel, and she'd scold you a little, and that would be the end of it. You must have thought of trying to get away, Bessie, didn't you?"

"Oh, I did, Miss Eleanor, often and often. When Jake was very bad, or Maw Hoover was meaner than usual. But it's just as you say. I was afraid that wherever I went it would be worse than it was there. I didn't know where to go or what to do."

"Well—that's so," said Dolly. "It must have been awfully hard. But then, how did you ever get the nerve to do it at all, Bessie? That's what I don't understand. The way you act now, it seems as if you always wanted to do just as you are told.''

''I thought you'd heard all about that, Dolly. You see, when we really did run away, we couldn't help it, Zara and I. And I don't believe we really meant to go quite away, the way we did —not at first. You remember when we saw you girls first—when you were in camp in the woods?''

''Oh, yes; I remember seeing you, with your head just poking out of the door of that funny old hut by the lake. I thought it was awfully funny, but I didn't know you then, of course.''

''I expect you'd have thought it was funny whether you knew us or not, Dolly. Well, you see, Zara had come over to see me the day it all happened, and Jake caught her talking with me, and locked her in the woodshed. Maw Hoover didn't like Zara, because she was a foreigner, and Maw thought she stole eggs and chickens—but

Zara never did such a thing in her life. So Jake locked her in the woodshed, and said that he was going to keep her there till Maw Hoover came home. She'd gone to town.''

"Why did he want to do that?''

"Because Maw had said that if she ever caught Zara around their place again she was going to take a stick to her and beat her until she was black and blue—and I guess she meant it, too. She liked to give people beatings—me, I mean. She never touched Jake, though, and she never believed he did anything wrong.''

Dolly whistled.

"If she knew him the way I do, she would,'' she said. "And I've only seen him twice—but that's two times too many!''

"Well, after he'd locked her in, Jake went off, and I tried to let her out. I couldn't find the key, and I was trying to break the lock on the door with a stone. I'd nearly got it done, when Jake came along and found me doing it. So he stood off and threw bits of burning wood from

the fire near me, to frighten me. That was an
old trick of his.

"But that time the woodshed caught fire, and
he was scared. He got the key, and we let Zara
out, and then he said he was going to tell Maw
Hoover that we'd set the place on fire on pur-
pose. I knew she'd believe him, and we were
frightened, and ran off."

"Well, I should say so! Who wouldn't? Why,
he's worse than I thought he was, even, and I
knew he was pretty bad."

"We were going to Zara's place first, but that
was the day they arrested Zara's father. They
said he'd been making bad money, but I don't
believe it. But anyhow, we heard them talking
in their place—Zara's and her father's—and they
said that I'd set the barn on fire, and they were
going to have me arrested, and that Zara would
have to go and live with old Farmer Weeks,
who's the meanest man in that state. And so
we kept on running away, because we knew that
it couldn't be any worse for us if we went than

if we stayed. So that's how we finally came away."

"Oh, how exciting! I wish I ever had adventures like that!"

"Don't be silly, Dolly," said Eleanor, severely. "Bessie and Zara were very lucky—they might have had a very hard time. And you had all the adventure you need the other day when you made Bessie go off looking for ice-cream sodas with you. You be content to go along the way you ought to and you'll have plenty of fun without the danger of adventures. They sound very nice, after they're all over, but when they're happening they're not very pleasant."

"That's so," admitted Dolly, becoming grave.

It was late in the afternoon before they reached the station at which they had to change from the main line. There they waited for a time before the little two-car train on the branch line was ready to start. Short and light as it was, that train had to be drawn by two puffing, snorting engines, for the rest of the trip was a climb, and

3—C4

a stiff one, since Long Lake was fairly high up,
though the train, after it passed the station nearest to the lake, would climb a good deal higher.

Even after they left the train finally, they were
still some distance from their destination.

"You needn't look at that buckboard as if you
were going to ride in it, girls," said Eleanor,
laughing, as they surveyed the single vehicle that
was waiting near the track. "That's just for the
baggage. Now you can see, maybe, why you
were told you couldn't bring many things with
you. And if that isn't enough, wait until you
see the trail!"

Soon all the baggage was stowed away on the
back of the buckboard and securely tied up, and
then the driver whipped up the stocky horses, and
drove off, while the girls gave him the Wohelo
cheer.

"But how are we going to get to Long Lake?"
asked Dolly, apprehensively.

"We're going to walk!" laughed Eleanor.
"Come on now or we won't get there in time for

supper—and I'll bet we'll all have a fine appetite for supper to-night!"

Then she took the van, and led the way across a field and into the woods that grew thickly near the track.

"This isn't the way the buckboard went!" said Dolly.

"No—we'll strike the road pretty soon, though," said Eleanor. "We save a little time by taking this trail. In the old days there wasn't any way to get to the lake, or to carry anything there, except by walking. And when they built the corduroy road they couldn't make it as short as the trail, although, wherever they could, they followed the old trail. So this is a sort of short cut."

"What's a corduroy road?" asked Dolly.

"Don't you know that? I though you knew something about the woods, Dolly. My, what a lot you've got to learn. It's made of logs and they're built in woods and places where it's hard to make a regular road, or would cost too much.

All that's needed, you see, is to chop down trees enough to make a clear path, and then to put down the logs, close together. It's rough going, and no wagon with springs can be driven over it, but it's all right for a buckboard."

"Ugh!" said Dolly. "I should think it would shake you to pieces."

"It does, pretty nearly," said Eleanor, with a smile. "One usually only rides over one once— after that one walks, and is glad of the chance."

When, after a three-mile tramp, Eleanor, who was in front, stopped suddenly at a point where the trees thinned out, on top of a ridge, and called out, "Here's the lake, girls!" there was a wild rush to reach her side. And the view, when they got the first glimpse of it, was certainly worth all the trouble it had caused them.

Before them stretched a long body of water, sapphire blue in the twilight, with pink shadows where the setting sun was reflected. Perhaps two miles long, the lake was, at its widest point, not more than a quarter of a mile across, whence,

of course, came its name. About it the land
sloped down on all sides, into a cup-like depres-
sion that formed the lake, so that there was, on
all four sides, a tree crowned ridge. From a
point about half way to the far end of the lake
smoke rose in the calm evening air.

"Oh, how beautiful!" cried Bessie. "It's the
loveliest place I ever saw. And how wonderful
the smell is."

"That's from the pine trees," said Eleanor.
She sighed, as if overcome by the calm beauty
of the scene, as, indeed, she was. "It's always
beautiful here—but sometimes I think it's most
beautiful in winter, when the lake is covered with
ice, and the trees are all weighed down with
snow. Then, of course, you can walk or skate
all over the lake—it's frozen four and five feet
deep, as a rule, by January."

Dolly shivered.

"But isn't it awfully cold here?" she inquired.

"Oh, yes; but it's so dry that one doesn't
mind the cold half as much as we do at home

when it's really ten or fifteen degrees warmer,
Dolly. One dresses for it, too, you see, in thick,
woolen things, and furs, and there's such glorious
sport. You can break holes through the ice and
fish, and then there are ice boats, and skating
races, and all sorts of things. Oh, it's glorious.
I've been up here in winter a lot, and I really do
think that's best of all.''

Then she looked at the rising smoke.

''Well, we mustn't stay here and talk any
more,'' she said. ''Come along, girls, it's getting
near to supper time.''

''Have we got to cook supper?'' asked Dolly,
anxiously.

''No, not to-night,'' said Eleanor, with a laugh.
''The guides have done it for us, because I knew
we'd all be tired and ready for a good rest, without any work to do. But with breakfast tomor-
row we'll start in and do all our own work, just
as we've done when we've been in camp before.''

Half an hour's brisk walk took them to the site
of the camp. There there was a little sandy beach,

and the tents had been pitched on ground that
was slightly higher. Behind each tent a trench
had been dug, so that, in case of rain, the water
flowing down from the high ground in the rear
would be diverted and carried down into the lake.

Before the tents a great fire was burning, and
the girls cried out happily at the sight of plates,
with knives and forks and tin pannikins set by
them, all spread out in a great circle near the fire.
At the fire itself two or three men were busy
with frying pans and great coffee pots, and the
savory smell of frying bacon, that never tastes
half as good as when it is eaten in the woods,
rose and mingled with the sweet, spicy smell of
the balsams and the firs, the pines and the
spruces.

"Oh, but I'm glad we're here!" cried Dolly,
with a huge sigh of content. "And I'm glad to
see supper—and smell it!"

And what a supper that was! For many of
the girls, like Bessie, and Zara, and Dolly, it was
the first woods meal. How good the bacon was,

and the raised biscuit, as light and flaky as
snowflakes, cooked as only woods guides know
how to cook them! And then, afterward, the great
plates heaped high with flapjacks, that were to
be eaten with butter and maple syrup that came
from the trees all about them. Not the adul-
terated, wishy-washy maple syrup that is sold, as
a rule, even in the best grocery stores of the
cities, but the real, luscious maple syrup that is
taken from the running sap in the first warm
days of February, and refined in great kettles,
right under the trees that yielded the sap.

And then, when it was time to turn in, how
they did sleep! The air seemed to have some
mysterious qualities of making one want to sleep.
And the peace of the great out-of-doors brooded
over the camp that night.

CHAPTER IV

In the morning, when the girls awoke, there was no sign of the guides who had cooked that tempting and delicious supper the night before.

"Well, we're on our own resources now, girls," said the Guardian. "This may be a sort of Eden —I hope we'll find it so. But it's going to be a manless one. There'll be no men here until we get ready to go away, if I can help it—except as visitors."

"Well, I guess we can get along without them all right, for a change," said Dolly, blushing a little.

"Some of the men I know who are interested in the Boy Scouts think the Camp Fire Girls are a good deal of a joke," said Eleanor, with a light in her eyes that might have made some of the scoffers she referred to anxious to eat their

57

words. "They say we get along all right because
we always have some man ready to help us out
if we get into any trouble. So I planned this
camp just to show them that we can do just as
well as any troop of Boy Scouts ever did."

"I bet we can, too," said Dolly, eagerly.
"Why, with such a lot of us to do the work,
it won't be very hard for any one of us."

"Not if we all do our share, Dolly," said
Eleanor, looking at her rather pointedly. "But
if some of us are always managing to disappear
just when there's work to be done, someone
will have to do double duty—and that's not
fair."

"I won't—really I won't, Miss Eleanor," said
Dolly. "I know I've shirked sometimes, but
I'm not going to this time. I'm going to
work hard now to be a Fire Maker. I think
I've been a Wood Gatherer long enough, don't
you?"

"You've served more time than is needed for
promotion, Dolly. It's all up to you, as the boys

say. As soon as you win the honors you need you can be a Fire Maker. You can have your new rank just as soon as you earn it."

"Bessie and I are going to be made Fire Makers together, if we can, Miss Eleanor. We talked that over the other day, at the farm, and I think we'll be ready at the first camp fire we have after we get home."

"Well, you'll please me very much if you do. It's time the other girls were getting up now—we've got to cook breakfast now. I'll call them while you two build a fire—there's plenty of wood for to-day, piled up over there."

As Dolly had said, with each girl doing her share, the work of the camp was light. While some of the girls did the cooking, others prepared the "dining table"—a smooth place on the ground—and others pinned up the bottom flaps of the tents, after turning out the bedding, so that the floors of the tents might be well aired. And then they all sat down, happily and hungrily, to a breakfast that tasted just as good as had supper the night before.

"Can we swim in the lake, Miss Eleanor?" asked Margery Burton.

"If you want to," said Eleanor, with a smile. "It's pretty cold water, though; a good deal colder than it was at the sea shore last year. You see, this lake is fed by springs, and in the spring the ice melts, and the water in April and May is just like ice water. But you'll get used to it, if you only stay in a couple of minutes at first, and get accustomed to the chill gradually. But remember the rule: no one is ever to go unless I'm right at hand, and there must always be someone in a boat, ready to help if a girl gets a cramp or any other sort of trouble."

"Oh, are there boats?" cried Dolly. "That's fine! Where are they, Miss Eleanor?"

"You shall see them after we've cleared away the breakfast things and washed up. But there's a rule about the boats, too: no one is to go out in them except in bathing suits. And remember this, when you're out on the lake. It's very narrow, and it looks very calm and safe, now.

"But at this time of the year there are often severe squalls up here, and they come over the hills so quickly that it's easy to get caught unless you're very careful. I think there had better always be two girls in each boat. We don't want any accidents."

"Can we go for walks through the woods, Miss Eleanor?"

"Oh, yes; that's the most beautiful part of being up here. But it's easy to get lost. When you start on a trail always stick to it. Don't be tempted to go off exploring. I'm going to give you all some lessons in finding your way in the woods. You know, the moss is always on the south side of a tree, and there are other ways of telling direction, by the leaves. I expect you all to be regular woodsmen when we go away from here, and I'm sure you'll learn things about the woods that will give you a good many pleasant times in the future."

"Isn't there anyone else at all up here, Miss Eleanor? I should think there'd be a hotel or something like that here."

' No, not yet; not right near here. This lake is part of a big preserve that is owned by a lot of men in the city. My father is one of them, and they have tried to keep all this part of the woods just as nature left it. There are a lot of deer here, and in the fall, when hunters come into the woods, they have to keep out of this part of them. A few deer are shot here, because if only a few are taken each year, it's all right. But there will be no hotels in this tract. Hotels mean the end of the real woods life. There are half a dozen lakes in the preserve, and each of the families that owns a share in it has a camp at one of the lakes. I mean a regular camp, with wooden buildings, where one can stay in the winter, even. But this lake was set apart for trips like this, where people can get right back to nature, and sleep in tents."

"Then we can go over and see some of the
other lakes?"

"Yes; I don't know whether we'll find anyone
at home in any of the camps or not, but they'll
be glad to see us if they are there. A lot of
people wait until later in the year to come up
here—until the hunting season begins. But we
can do some hunting even now, though it's
against the law to do any shooting."

"Oh, I know what you mean, Miss Eleanor—
with a camera?"

It was Margery Burton who thought of that.

"Yes. And that's really the best sort of hunting, I think. If you've ever seen a deer, and had
it look at you with its big, soft eyes, I don't see
how you can kill it. It's almost as hard to get
a good picture of a deer as it is to kill it—in fact,
I think it's harder, because you have to get so
much closer to it. And it's awfully good fun at
night.

"You go to one of their runways, and settle
down, with your camera and a flashlight powder,

and then when the deer comes, if you're very quick, you can get a really beautiful picture. The deer may be a little frightened, but he isn't hurt, and you have a picture that you can keep for years and show to people. And an experienced hunter will tell you that any time you can get close enough to a deer to get a good flashlight picture of him you could easily have killed him.''

''Why is it so very hard to do that?''

''Well, for lots of reasons. You have to figure on the wind—because if the wind is blowing away from you and toward the deer he can smell you long before he's in sight, and off he goes, afraid to come any nearer.''

''But how can you tell where a deer will be?''

''They have regular runways—just as we have trails. And at night they come down to the lake to drink. So you can station yourself on one of those runways, and be pretty sure that sooner or later a deer will come along.''

The morning passed quickly and happily. To the girls who had never before been in that country, there seemed to be an unending number of new discoveries. Timid as the deer might be, there was nothing nervous about the squirrels and chipmunks which abounded in the woods near the lake, and as soon as they saw the girls they came running about, so that there were often half a dozen or more begging noisily for dainties to afford them a change from their diet of nuts, sitting up, and chattering prettily as they got the morsels that were tossed to them.

"I never saw them so tame, even at home," said Bessie, surprised. "We had plenty of them there, but I suppose they were wilder because the boys used to shoot them. They don't do that here, I suppose?"

"No; the people who hunt around here go in for bigger game. They would think they were wasting their time if they bothered to shoot chipmunks and squirrels."

"I've seen them tame before, but that was in the park, at home, and it isn't the same thing at all," said Dolly.

"No; though they're very cute, and I'm **glad** there are so many of them there. But here, of course, they're in their real home, and it's different, and much nicer, I think."

Then, after luncheon, Miss Eleanor divided the girls into watches.

"I think we'll have more fun if a certain number stay home every afternoon to prepare dinner and cook it," she said. "Then the rest of you can go for walks, or do anything you like, so long as you are back in time for dinner. In that way, some of you will be free every afternoon, and those who have to work won't mind, because they will know that the next day they will be free, and so on."

Zara was one of those who drew a piece of paper marked "work" from the big hat in which Miss Eleanor put a slip of paper for every girl, while Bessie and Dolly each drew a slip marked "play."

"To-morrow the girls who work to-day will play," said Miss Eleanor, "and those who play to-day will draw again. Four of them will play again to-morrow, and the other four will work, and then, on the third day, those who play to-morrow will work, and on the fourth day to-day's four will work again. That will give everyone two days off and one day to work while we're in camp. And I think that's fair."

So did everyone else, and Dolly, always willing to put off work as long as she could, was delighted.

"Let's take a long walk this afternoon, Bessie," she said. "The air up here makes me feel more like walking than I ever do when I'm at home. There I usually take a car whenever I can, though I've been trying to walk more lately, so as to get an honor bead."

"I'll be glad to take a walk, Dolly," said Bessie, laughing. "I think you ought to be encouraged any time you really want to do something that's good for you."

"Oh, if I stay with you long enough I'll be too good to keep on living," said Dolly. "Don't you see the difference between us, Bessie? You're

good because you like to do the things you ought
to do. And when anyone tells me something's
good for me, I always get so that I don't want
to do it. We'll start right after lunch, shall
we?''

"All right," said Bessie.

But before it was time to make a start she
sought out Miss Eleanor.

"I'm not really afraid, Wanaka,'" she said,
using the Indian name, since, here in the woods,
it seemed natural to do it. "But I thought I ought
to ask you if you think it's all right for me to go
off with Dolly? I suppose none of those people
who were trying to get hold of me would do anything up here, would they?''

"Oh, I don't think so, Bessie. No, I think
you're just as safe anywhere in these woods as
you would be right here in the camp. There are
a few guides around—they have to be kept here
to warn people who make camp and don't put
out their fires properly. You see, my father and
the rest of the people don't mind letting nice peo-

ple come here into their preserve to camp, but they've got to be careful about fire.

"You can imagine what would happen here if the woods caught fire; it would be dreadful. Further on, the woods are only just beginning to grow up again. They were all burned out a year or so ago, and they look horrid. This preserve is so beautiful that we all want to keep it looking just as nice as possible. But the guides would look after you; there's nothing to be afraid of with them.

"And I don't believe that you'd be at all likely to meet anyone else. Suppose you take the trail that starts at the far end of the lake, and follow it straight over until you come to Little Bear Lake. That's a very pretty walk. But don't go off the preserve. There's a trail that leads over to Loon Pond, but you'd better not try that until we all go as a party."

So, when the midday meal had been eaten, Bessie and Dolly started off, skirting the edge of the lake until they came to the beginning of the trail Miss Mercer had spoken of, which was marked by a birch bark sign on a tree. There they left the lake, and plunged so quickly into thick woods that the water was soon out of sight.

"Isn't this lovely? Oh, I could walk miles and miles here and never get tired at all, I believe!" said Dolly. "But I do sort of wish there was a hotel somewhere around. They have dances, and parties, and all sorts of fun at those hotels. And, Bessie, do you know I heard there was one near here, at a place called Loon Pond?"

"Is there?"

"Yes; I think it would be fun to go there some time."

"Well, maybe we can, some time, Dolly. When Miss Eleanor is along. But we'd better not do it today. You know she said we were to stick to the preserve."

"Oh, bother; as if we could get into any mischief up here! But I suppose there wouldn't be any use in trying to persuade you; you always do just as you're told."

"Oh, I'd like to see the hotel, too, Dolly, but not today. The woods are enough for me now. And we can go there some other time, I'm sure."

Dolly said nothing more just then, and for a time they walked along quietly.

"We're about half way to Little Bear Lake now," announced Dolly, after a spell of silence.

"Why, how do you know?"

"Because I saw a map, and this ridge we've just come to is half way between the two lakes."

"Oh," said Bessie.

"Yes. We've been coming up hill so far now, the rest of the way is down hill, so it will be easier walking."

"That's good; it means that when we're going home we'll be going down for the last half of the trip, when we're tired. That's much easier than if it was the other way, I think."

"You look tired, Bessie; why don't you sit down and rest?"

"Well, that's not a bad idea, Dolly. I'm not used to so much walking lately."

"All right, sit down. I'm thirsty. I think I'll just run ahead and see if I can find a spring while you rest."

So Dolly ran ahead, and disappeared after a moment. Presently, when Bessie was rested, she started again, and soon overtook Dolly.

"We turn here," said Dolly. "See, here's another trail, and the signs show which one we're to take."

"That's funny," said Bessie, puzzled. "I thought we went to Little Bear in a perfectly straight line. Miss Eleanor didn't say anything about changing direction."

"Well, there's the sign, Bessie. If we keep straight on it says that we'll come to Loon Pond. We turn off to the right here to get to Little Bear."

"Well, I guess the sign must be right. But it certainly seems funny. I hope there isn't any mistake."

"Mistake? How can there be? Don't be silly, Bessie. There wouldn't be any chance of that. Come on."

So they turned off, and, as they followed the new trail, the trees began to grow thinner, presently. The whole character of the woods seemed to change, too. They passed numerous places where picnic parties had evidently eaten their meals, and had left blackened spots, and the remnants of their feasts.

"It seems to me some of the people who've been here have been very careless, Dolly," said Bessie. "Look, there's a place where a fire started. It didn't get very far, but it burnt over quite a little bit of ground before it was put out."

The trail began to dip sharply, too, and before long they were walking in what was almost open country. Stumps of trees were all about, and evidently wood-cutters had been at work.

"This isn't half as pretty as Long Lake," said Bessie. "Oh, Dolly, look! What's that?"

Dolly laughed in a peculiar fashion. For they

had come in sight of a sheet of water, and, in plain view, not far from them, by the shore of the lake, they saw a place that could not be mistaken. It proclaimed its nature at once—a regular summer hotel, with wide piazzas, full of people. And on the water there were a score of boats and canoes, and one or two launches.

"This isn't Little Bear Lake!" said Bessie.

"Of course it isn't, silly; it's Loon Pond. I changed the signs while you rested, because I meant to come here, and I knew you wouldn't, if you knew what you were doing!"

CHAPTER V

Bessie grew red with indignation for a moment, but before she spoke she was calm again.

"Don't you think that's a pretty mean trick, Dolly?" she said, gently. "It seems to me it's a good deal like lying."

"Why, Bessie King! Can't you ever take a joke? I didn't say a single, solitary thing that wasn't so. I said the signs said this was the way to Little Bear Lake, and you never asked me if I'd changed them, did you?"

Bessie laughed helplessly.

"Oh, Dolly!" she said. "Of course I didn't; why should I? Who would ever think of doing such a thing, except you? You don't expect people to guess what you're going to do next, do you?"

"I suppose not," said Dolly, impenitently, her

75

eyes still twinkling. "I do manage to surprise people pretty often. My aunt Mabel says that if I spent half as much time studying as I do thinking up new sorts of mischief I'd be at the top of every class I'm in at school."

"She's perfectly right. I thought at first you had a hard time with your aunt, Dolly, but I'm through being sorry for you. She needs all the sympathy anyone has got for having to try to look after you!"

"Oh, what's the harm? We're here now, and it isn't so very dreadful, is it? Come on, let's go over to the hotel."

"Indeed we shan't do anything of the sort, Dolly Ransom! We'll turn around and go right straight back to Long Lake, that's what we'll do."

"I guess not. You don't think I've come this far and that I'm going to turn around without seeing what the place is like, do you?"

"Why, Dolly, you know we weren't supposed to come here alone. I don't think much of it; it

isn't half as pretty as Long Lake. What's the
use of wasting our time here, anyhow?''

"Why—why—because there are people here!
I just love seeing people, Bessie, they're so in-
teresting, because they're all so different, and
you never know what they're going to say or do.
And there may be someone we know here, too.''

"There can't be anyone I know, Dolly.''

"Oh, bother! Well, there may be someone I
know, and that's the same thing, isn't it? Come
on, be a sport, Bessie.''

"That's what you said about going in the car
with Mr. Holmes the other day, too.''

"Oh, but this isn't a bit like that, Bessie.''

"It might get us into just as much mischief,
Dolly. No, I'm not going over there. It's silly,
and it's wrong.''

And this time Bessie stood firm. Despite
Dolly's pleading, which turned, presently, to
angry threats, she refused absolutely to go any
nearer the hotel, and Dolly was afraid to venture there alone, though there was very little she

was afraid to *do*. In her inmost heart, of course, Dolly knew that Bessie was right, and that she had had no business to trick her chum into seeming to break her promise to Miss Eleanor.

"Oh, well," she said, "I might have known that I couldn't always make you do what you don't want to do, Bessie. You're not mad at me, are you?"

Bessie, pleased by this sign of surrender, returned the smile.

"I ought to be, but I'm not, Dolly," she answered. "I think that is one of the reasons you keep on doing these things—but no one ever really does get angry with you, as they should. If someone you really cared for got properly angry at you just once for one of your little tricks, I think it would teach you not to do anything of the sort for a long time."

"Oh, I don't mean any harm, Bessie, and you know it, and when people really like you they don't get angry unless they think you're really trying to be mean. I say, Bessie, if you won't go

over to the hotel, will you walk just a little way
over to the other side, and see what that funny
looking place is where those big wagons are all
spread out?"

Bessie followed Dolly's pointing finger, and
saw, on the side of Loon Pond opposite the hotel,
several wagons, among which smoke was rising.

"It looks like a circus," said Dolly.

"It isn't, though. I know what they are," said
Bessie, promptly. "It's a gypsy encampment.
Do you mean you've never seen one, Dolly?"

"No; and oh dear, Bessie, I've always wanted
to. Surely we could go a little nearer, couldn't
we? As long as we're here?"

Bessie thought it over for a moment, and, as a
matter of fact, really could see no harm in spend-
ing ten minutes or so in walking over toward the
gypsy camp. She herself had seen a few gypsies
near Hedgeville in her time, but in that part of
the country those strange wanderers were not
popular.

"All right," she said. "But if I do that will

you promise to start for home as soon as we've had a look at them, and never to play such a trick on me again?''

"I certainly will. Bessie, you're a darling. And I'll tell you something else; too; you were so nice about the way I changed those signs that I'm really sorry I did it. And I just thought it would be a good joke. Usually I'm glad when people get angry at my jokes, it shows they were good ones.''

Bessie smiled wisely to herself. Gradually she was learning that the way to rob Dolly's jokes and teasing tricks of their sting, and the best way, at the same time, to cure Dolly herself of her fondness for them, was never to let the joker know that they had had the effect she planned.

Dolly, considerably relieved, as a matter of fact, when she found that Bessie was really not angry at her for the trick she had played with the sign post, chatted volubly as they turned to walk over toward the gypsy camp.

"I don't see why they call this a pond and the one we're on a lake," she said. "This is ever so much bigger than Long Lake. Why, it must be four or five miles long, don't you think, Bessie?"

"Yes. I guess they call it a pond because it looks just like a big, overgrown ice pond. See, it's round. I think Long Lake is ever so much prettier, don't you, even though it's smaller?"

"I certainly do. This place isn't like the woods at all, it's more like regular country, that you can find by just taking a trolley car and riding a few miles out from the city."

"It used to be just as it is now around Long Lake, I suppose," said Bessie. "But they've cut the trees down, and made room for tennis courts and all sorts of things like that, and then, I suppose, they needed wood to build the hotel, too. It's quite a big place, isn't it, Dolly?"

"Yes, and I've heard of it before, too," said Dolly. "A friend of mine stayed up here for a month two or three years ago. She says they advertise that it's wild and just like living right in the woods, but it isn't at all. I guess it's for people who like to think they're roughing it when they're really just as comfortable as they would be if they stayed at home. Comfortable the same way, I mean.''

''Yes, that's better, Dolly. Because I think we're comfortable, though it's very different from the way we would live in the city, or even from the way we lived at the farm. But we're really roughing it, I guess.''

''Yes, and it's fine, too! Tell me, Bessie, did you ever see any gypsies like these when you lived in the country?''

''There were gypsies around Hedgeville two or three times, but the farmers all hated them, and used to try to drive them away, and Maw Hoover told me not to go near them when they were around. She usually gave me so many things to do that I couldn't, anyhow. You know, the farmers say that they'll steal anything, but I think one reason for that is that the farmers drove

them into doing it, in the beginning, I mean.
They wouldn't let them act like other people, and
they didn't like to sell them things. So I think
the poor gypsies wanted to get even, and that's
how they began to steal.''

''What do you suppose they're doing up here,
Bessie?''

''They always go around to the summer places,
and in the winter they go south, to where the
people from the north go to get warm when it's
winter at home. They tell fortunes, and they
make all sorts of queer things that people like to
buy; lace, and bead things. And I suppose up
here they sell all sorts of souvenirs, too; baskets,
and things like that.''

''Don't they have any real homes, Bessie?''

''No; except in their wagons. They live in
them all the time, and they always manage to be
where it's warm in the winter. They don't care
where they go, you see. One place is just like
another to them. They never have settled in
towns. They've been wanderers for ages and

ages, and they have their own language. They know all sorts of things about the weather, and they can find their way anywhere.''

''How do you know so much about them, Bessie, if you never saw anything of them when you were in Hedgeville?''

''I read a book about them once. It's called 'Lavengro,' and it's by a man who's been dead a long time now; his name was Borrow.''

''What a funny name! I never heard of that book, but I'll get it and read it when I get home. It tells about the gypsies, you say?''

''Yes. But I guess not about the gypsies as they are now, but more as they used to be. We're getting close, now. See all the babies! Aren't they cute and brown?''

Two or three parties, evidently from the hotel, were looking about the camp, but they paid little attention to the two Camp Fire Girls, evidently recognizing that they did not come from the hotel. The gypsies, however, always on the alert when they see a chance to make money by selling their wares or by telling fortunes, flocked about them, particularly the women. Bessie, fair haired and blond, they seemed disposed to neglect, but Bessie noticed that several of the men looked admiringly at Dolly, whose dark hair and eyes, though she was, of course, much fairer than their own women, seemed to appeal to them.

"I'd like to have my fortune told!" Dolly whispered.

"I think we'd better not do that, Dolly, really; and you remember you said you'd stay just for a minute."

"I don't see what harm it would do," Dolly pouted. But she gave in, nevertheless. They passed the door of the strangely decorated tent inside of which the secrets of the future were supposed to be revealed, and, followed by a curious pack of children, walked on to a wagon where a pretty girl, who seemed no older than themselves but was probably, because the gypsy women grow old so much more quickly than American girls, actually younger, was sitting. She was sewing beads to a jacket, and she looked up with a bright smile as they approached.

"You come from the hotel?" she said. "You live there?"

"No," said Dolly. "We come from a long way off. Are you going to wear that jacket?"

The gypsy girl laughed.

"No. I'm making that for my man, him over there by the tree, smoking, see? He's my man; he's goin' marry me when I get it done."

Bessie laughed.

"Marry you? Why, you're only a girl like me!" she exclaimed.

"No, no; me woman," protested the gypsy, eagerly. "See, I'm so tall already!"

And she sprang up to show them how tall she was. But Bessie and Dolly only laughed the more, until Bessie saw that something like anger was coming into her black eyes, and checked Dolly's laugh.

"I hope you'll be very happy," she said. "Come on, Dolly, we really must be going."

Dolly was inclined to resist once more. She hadn't seen half as much as she wanted to of the strange, exotic life of the gypsy caravan, so different from the things she was used to, but Bessie was firm, and they began to make their way back toward the trail. And, as they neared the spot from which they had had their first view of Loon Pond and the gypsy camp, Bessie was startled and frightened by the sudden appearance in their path of the good looking young gypsy for whom the girl they had been talking to was decorating the jacket.

His keen eyes devoured Dolly as he stood before her, and he put out his hand, gently enough, to bar their way.

"Will you marry me?" he said, in English much better than that of most of his tribe.

Dolly laughed, although Bessie looked serious.

"Oh, yes, of course," said Dolly. "I always marry the first man who asks me, every day; especially if he's a gypsy and I've never seen him before."

"You're too young now; you think you are, I suppose," said the gypsy, showing his white teeth. "You come back with me and wait; by and by we will get married."

"Nonsense," said Bessie, decisively. "He means it, Dolly, he's not joking. Come, we must hurry."

"Wait, stay," said the gypsy, eagerly. And he put out his hand as if to hold Dolly. But she screamed before he could touch her, and darted past him. And in a moment both girls, running hard, were out of sight.

CHAPTER VI

A SERIOUS JOKE

Bessie, seriously alarmed, led the race through
the woods and they had gone for nearly a quarter
of a mile before she would even stop to listen.
When she felt that if the gypsy were going to
overtake them he would have done it, she stopped,
and, breathing hard, listened eagerly for some
sign that he was still behind them. But only the
noises of the forest came to their ears, the rustling
of the leaves in the trees, the call of a bird, the
sudden sharp chattering of a squirrel or a chip-
munk, and, of course, their own breathing.

"I guess we got away from him all right," she
said. "Oh, Dolly, I was frightened!"

"What?" cried Dolly, amazed. "Do you mean
to say that you let that silly gypsy frighten you?
I thought you were braver than that, Bessie!"

"You don't know anything about it, Dolly,"

89

said Bessie, a little irritated. "It really wasn't your fault, but those people aren't like our men. He probably meant just what he said, and if he thought you were laughing at him, it would have made him furious. When you said you would marry him, of course I knew you were joking, and so would anyone like us, but I think he took you seriously. He thought you meant it!"

"Bessie! How absurd! He couldn't! Why, I won't marry anyone for ever so long, and he surely doesn't think an American girl would ever marry one of his nasty tribe! You're joking, aren't you? He couldn't ever have really thought anything so perfectly absurd?"

"I only hope we won't find out that he was serious, Dolly. You couldn't be expected to understand, but people like that are very different from ourselves. They haven't got a lot of civilized ideas to hold them in check, the way we have, and when they want something they come right out and say so, and if they can't get what they want by asking for it, they're apt to take it."

"But I didn't think anyone ever acted like that! And he is going to marry that pretty gypsy girl who is putting the beads and buttons on a jacket for him, anyhow. She said so; she said they were engaged."

"Men have changed their minds about the women they were going to marry, Dolly, even American men. And that's another thing that bothers me. I think that girl's very much in love with him, and if she thought he was fond of you, she'd be furious. There's no telling what a gypsy girl might do if she was jealous. You see, she'd blame you, instead of him. She'd say you had turned his head."

"Oh, Bessie, what a dreadful mess. Oh, dear! I seem to be getting into trouble all the time! I think I'm just going to have a little harmless fun and then I find that I've started all sorts of trouble that I couldn't foresee at all."

"Never mind, Dolly. You didn't mean to do it, and, of course, I may be exaggerating it anyhow. I'll admit I'm frightened, but it's because

of what I know about the gypsies. They're
strange people and they carry a grudge a long
time. If they think anyone has hurt them, or
offended them, they're never satisfied until they
have had their revenge. But, after all, he may
not do anything at all. He may have been joking.
Perhaps he just wanted to frighten you."

"Oh, I really do think that must have been it,
Bessie. Don't you remember that he was different from the others? He spoke just as well as
we do, as if he'd been to school, and he must know
more about our customs."

Bessie shook her head.

"That doesn't mean that he isn't just as wild
and untamed as the others down at bottom,
Dolly. I've heard the same thing about Indians;
that some of those who make the most trouble
are the very ones who've been to Carlisle. It
isn't because they're educated, because they
would have been wild and wicked anyhow, but
the very fact that they are educated seems to
make them more dangerous. I hope it isn't the

same with this gypsy; but we've got to be careful."

"Oh, I'll be careful, Bessie," said Dolly, with a shudder. "I'll do whatever I'm told. You needn't worry about that."

"That's good, Dolly. The first thing, of course, is never to get far away from the camp alone. We mustn't come over this way at all, or go anywhere near Loon Pond as long as those gypsies are still there."

"Oh, Bessie, do you think we'll have to tell Miss Eleanor about this?"

"I'm afraid so, Dolly. But there's no reason why you should mind doing that. She won't blame you, it really wasn't your fault."

"Yes, it was, Bessie. Don't you remember the way I changed the signs? If I hadn't done that we wouldn't have gone to Loon Pond, and if we hadn't gone there—"

"We wouldn't have seen the gypsies? Yes, I know, Dolly. But Miss Eleanor is fair, you know that. And she may scold you for playing the

trick with the signs, but that's all. She won't
blame you for having misunderstood that
gypsy.''

Then they came to the crossing of the trails,
and Dolly replaced the signs as they had been before she had played her thoughtless prank.

"We must hurry along, Dolly," said Bessie.
"It's getting dark, and we don't want to be out
here when it's too dark. I think it's safe enough,
but—"

"Oh, suppose that horrid gypsy followed us
through the woods, Bessie? That's what you
mean, isn't it? Let's get back to the camp just
as fast as ever we can."

"Bessie, I'm an awful coward, I'm afraid,"
Dolly said, as the camp was approached. "Will
you tell Miss Eleanor what happened; everything?
I'm afraid that if I told her myself I wouldn't
put in what I did with the signs."

"You wouldn't tell her a story, Dolly?"

"No, but I might just not tell her that. You
see, I wouldn't have really to tell her a story,

and, oh, Bessie, I want her to know all about it.
Then if she scolds me, all right. Can't you understand?''

''I'll do it if you like, Dolly, but I'm quite sure
you'd tell her everything yourself. You're not a
bit of a·coward, Dolly, because when you've done
something wrong you never try to pretend that
it was the fault of someone else, or an accident.''

''Do you think I ought to tell Miss Eleanor myself?'' said Dolly, wistfully. ''I will if you say
so, Bessie, but I'd much rather not.''

''No, I'll tell her,'' Bessie decided. ''I think
you're mistaken about yourself, Dolly, and the
reason I'm going to tell her is because I think
you'd make her think you were worse than you
were, instead of not telling her the whole thing.
Do you see?''

''You're ever so good, Bessie. Really, I'm going to try to stop worrying you so much after
this. It seems to me that you're always having
things to bother you on account of me.''

Miss Eleanor, at first, like Dolly, was inclined to laugh at what Bessie told her of the gypsy and his absurd suggestion that Dolly should stay with his tribe until she was old enough to be married to him.

"Why, he must have been joking, Bessie," she said. "You say he talked well; as if he were educated? Then he surely knows that no American girl would take such an idea seriously for a moment."

"But American girls do live with the gypsies and marry them, Miss Eleanor. Often, I've heard of that. And if you'd seen him when he got in our way on the trail you'd know why he frightened me. His face was perfectly black, he was so angry. And when Dolly laughed at him he looked as if he would like to beat her."

"I can understand that," laughed Miss Eleanor. "I've wanted to beat Dolly myself sometimes when she laughed when she was being scolded for something!"

"Oh, but this was different," said Bessie,

earnestly. "Really, Miss Eleanor, you'd have been frightened too, if you'd seen him. And I do think Dolly ought to be very careful until they've gone away from Loon Pond."

Bessie was so serious that Miss Eleanor was impressed, almost despite herself.

"Well, yes, she must be careful, of course. I don't want the girls going over to Loon Pond, anyway. I want them to have this time in the woods, and live in a natural way, and the Loon Pond people at the hotel just spoil the woods for me. But I don't believe there's any reason for being really frightened, Bessie."

"Suppose that man tried to carry her off?"

"Oh, he wouldn't dare to try anything like that, Bessie. I don't believe the gypsies are half as bad as they are painted, anyhow, but, even if he would be willing to do it, he'd be afraid. The guides would soon run him out of the preserve if they found him here; no one is supposed to be on it, without permission. And a gypsy couldn't get that, I know."

"But it's a pretty big place, and there aren't so very many guides. We didn't see one today, and we really took quite a long walk."

"But, Bessie, what would he do with her if he did carry her off? Those people travel along the roads, and they travel slowly. He must know that if anything happened to Dolly, or if she disappeared, he'd be suspected right away, and he'd be chased everywhere he went."

"I think it would be easy to hide someone in their caravans, though, Miss Eleanor. And those people stick together, so that no one would betray him if he did anything like that. We might be perfectly sure that he had done it, but we wouldn't be able to prove it."

"I'll speak to the guides and have them keep a good watch in the direction of Loon Pond, Bessie. There, will that make you feel any better? And those gypsies won't stay over there very long. They never do."

"Have they been here before, Miss Eleanor?"

"Oh, yes; every year when I've been here."

"Well, I'll feel better when they've gone, Miss Eleanor."

"So will I. You've made me quite nervous, Bessie. I think you'd better tell Dolly, and be careful yourself, not to tell the other girls anything about this. There's no use in scaring them, and making them feel nervous, too."

"No. I thought of that, too. Some of them would be frightened, I'm sure. I think Zara would be. She's been very nervous, anyhow, ever since we got her away from that awful house where Mr. Holmes had hidden her away from us."

"I don't blame her a bit; I would be, too. It was really a dreadful experience, Bessie, and particularly because she knew it was, in a way, her own fault."

"You mean because she believed what they said about being her friends, and that she would get you and me into trouble unless she went with them that night when they came for her?"

"Yes. Poor Zara! I'm afraid she guessed,

somehow, that I had been angry with her, at first.
She's terribly sensitive, and she seems to be able
to guess what's in your mind when you've really
scarcely thought the things yourself.''

''Well, I think it will be a good thing if she
doesn't know about this gypsy trouble, Miss
Eleanor. So I'll go and find Dolly, and tell her
not to say anything.''

''Do, Bessie. And get Dolly to come to me before dinner. She was wrong to play that trick
with the signs, but I don't mean to scold her. I
want to comfort her, instead. I think she's been
punished enough already, if she's really frightened about that gypsy.''

Dolly seemed to be a good deal chastened after
her talk with Eleanor, and Bessie felt glad that
the Guardian, though she evidently did not take
the episode of the gypsy as seriously as did Bessie, had still thought it worth while to let Dolly
think she did.

''I'm going to stay close to the camp after this,
Bessie,'' she said. ''And, oh, Miss Eleanor said

that there were footprints this morning near the water that a deer must have made. I've got my camera here; suppose we try to get a picture of one tonight? We could go to sleep early, and then get up. Miss Eleanor said it would be all right, just for the two of us. She said if any more sat up it would frighten the deer."

"All right," agreed Bessie. "That would be lots of fun."

So they slept for an hour or so, and then, about midnight, got up and went down to the shore of the lake, to a spot where a narrow trail came out of the woods. There they hid themselves behind some brush and placed Dolly's camera and a flashlight powder, to be ready in case the deer appeared.

They waited a long time. But at last there was a rustling in the trees, and they could hear the branches being pushed aside as some creature made its way slowly toward the water.

"All ready, Bessie?" whispered Dolly. "When I give you a squeeze press that button; that will set the flashlight off, and I'll take the picture as you do it.''

They waited tensely, and Bessie was as excited as Dolly herself. She felt as if she could scarcely wait for the signal. Dolly held her left hand loosely, and two or three times she thought the grip was tightening. But the signal came at last, and there was a blinding flash. But it was not a deer which stood out in the glare; it was the gypsy who had pursued Dolly!

CHAPTER VII

A THIEF IN THE NIGHT

The glare of the explosion lasted for only a moment. Dolly's eyes were fixed on the camera, as she bent her head down, and Bessie realized, thankfully, that she had not seen the evil face of the gypsy. As for the man, he cried out once, but the sound of his voice was drowned by the noise of the explosion. And then, as soon as the flashlight powder had burned out, the light was succeeded by a darkness so black that no one could have seen anything, so great was the contrast between it and the preceding illumination.

"Come, Dolly! Quick! Don't stop to argue! Run!" urged Bessie.

She seized Dolly's hand in hers, and made off, running down by the lake, and, for a few steps, actually through the water. Her one object was to get back to the camp as quickly as possible.

103

She thought, and the event proved that she was right, the gypsy, if he saw them nearing the camp fire, which was still burning brightly, would not dare to follow them very closely.

He had no means of knowing that there were no men in the camp, and, while he might not have been afraid to follow them right into camp had he known that, Bessie judged correctly that he would take no more chances than were necessary.

"Bessie, are you crazy?" gasped Dolly, as they came into the circle of light from the fire. "My feet are all wet! Whatever is the matter with you? You nearly made me smash my camera!"

"I don't care," said Bessie, panting, but immensely relieved. "Sit down here by the fire and take off your shoes and stockings; they'll soon get dry. I'm going to do it."

She was as good as her word, and not until they had dried their feet and set the shoes and stockings to dry would she explain what had caused her wild dash from the scene of the trap they had laid for the deer, and which had so nearly proved to be a trap for them, instead.

"If you'd looked up when that powder went off you'd have run yourself, Dolly, without being made to do it," she said, then. "That wasn't a deer we heard, Dolly."

"What was it, a bear or some sort of a wild animal?"

"No, it was a man."

Dolly's face was pale, even in the ruddy glow of the fire.

"You don't mean—it wasn't—"

"The gypsy? Yes, that's just who it was, Dolly. He's found out somehow where we are, you see. It's just what I was afraid of, that he would manage to follow us over here. But I'm not afraid now, as long as we know he's around. I don't see how he can possibly do you any harm."

"Oh, Bessie, what a lucky, lucky thing that we saw him! If we hadn't just happened to try to get that picture we would never have done it.

The nasty brute! The idea of his daring to follow us over here. Do you think he would have
really tried to carry me back to his tribe, Bessie?"

"I don't know, Dolly. His face looked awful
when I saw it in the glare. But then, of course,
he was terribly surprised. He probably thought
he was the only soul awake for miles and miles,
and to have that thing go off in one's face would
startle anybody, and make them look pretty
scary."

"I should say so! You have to pucker up your
face and shut your eyes. Do you think he saw
us, Bessie?"

"I shouldn't think it was very likely, Dolly.
You see, it's just as you say. The glare of a
flashlight is blinding, when it goes off suddenly
like that, right in front of you. I don't think
you're likely to see much of anything except the
glare. And, of course, he hadn't the slightest reason to be expecting to see us. I expect he's more
puzzled and frightened than we are; he's certainly a good deal more puzzled."

"Then maybe he'll be so frightened that he'll go back to his people and let me alone, Bessie."

"I certainly hope so, Dolly. It really doesn't seem possible that he'd dare to carry you off, even if he could get hold of you. He'd know that we'd be sure to suspect that he was the one who had done it, and even a gypsy ought to know what happens to people who do things like that. I don't see how he could hope to escape."

"But, Bessie, I was thinking: suppose he didn't carry me to the place where the other gypsies are? Suppose he took me right off into the woods somewhere, and hid?"

"You'd both have to have food, Dolly. And as he couldn't get that very easily, he'd be taking a big chance of getting caught. No, what I really think is that he wants to see you, and try to persuade you to go with him willingly. Then he wouldn't be in any danger, you see."

"Ugh! He must be an awful fool to think he could do that!"

"Well, he's not bad looking, Dolly. And he's

probably vain. The chances are that all the
gypsy girls set their caps at him, because, if you
remember, he was about the only good looking
young man there in their camp. Most of the men
were married. So, if he's always been popular
with the girls of his own people, he may have
got the idea that he's quite irresistible. That all
he's got to do is to tell a girl he wants to marry
her to have her fall right into his arms, like a
ripe apple falling from a tree.''

''The horrid brute! If he ever comes near
me again, I'll slap his face for him.''

''You'd better not do anything of the sort.
The best thing for you to do if you ever see him
anywhere near you again is to run, just as hard
as you can. Dolly, you've no idea of the rage a
man like that can fly into. If you struck him you
can't tell what he might try to do. But I hope
you'll never see him again.''

Dolly shivered a little.

''Are you sleepy, Bessie?'' she asked.

''No, I think I'm too excited to be sleepy. It

was so startling to be expecting to see a deer, and then to see his face in the light. No, I'm not sleepy."

"Oh, Bessie! Isn't it possible that you were mistaken? You know, you couldn't have seen his face for more than a moment, if you did see it. Weren't you thinking so much of that gypsy that you just fancied you saw him, when you really didn't at all?"

"No, no, I'm quite sure, Dolly. I was perfectly certain it was a deer, and that was all I was thinking about. And I heard him cry out, too. That would be enough to make me certain that I was right. A deer wouldn't have cried out, and it wouldn't have stood perfectly still, either. It would have turned around and run as soon as it saw the light; any animal would have. It would have been too terrified to do anything else."

"But don't you suppose he was frightened? Why didn't he run?"

"Were you ever so frightened that you couldn't do a thing but just stand still? I have been; so frightened that I couldn't even have cried out for help, and couldn't have moved for a minute or so, for anything in the world.

"I think he may have been frightened that way. Men aren't like animals, they're more likely to be too frightened to move than to run away because they're afraid. And the fear that makes a man run away is a different sort, anyhow."

"It's getting cold, isn't it?"

"Yes, the fire's burning low. We'd better get to bed, Dolly."

"Oh, no; I couldn't. I don't want to be there in the dark. I'm sure I couldn't sleep if I went to bed. I'd much rather sit out here by the fire and talk, if you're not sleepy. And you said you weren't."

"I suppose we could get some more wood and throw it on the fire. It would be warm enough then, if we got a couple of blankets to wrap around us."

"I think it's a good idea to stay awake and keep watch, anyhow, in case he should come back.

Then, if he saw someone sitting up by the fire
he would be scared off, I should think.''

''All right. Slip in as quietly as you can, Dolly,
and get our blankets from the tent, while I put
on some more wood. There's lots of it, that's a
good thing. There's no reason why we shouldn't
use it.''

So, while Dolly crept into their tent to get the
blankets, Bessie piled wood high on the embers
of the camp fire, until the sparks began to fly, and
the wood began to burn with a high, clear flame.
And when Dolly returned she had with her a box
of marshmallows.

''Now we'll have a treat,'' she said. ''I forgot all about these. I didn't remember I'd
brought them with me. Give me a pointed stick
and I'll toast you one.''

Bessie looked on curiously. The joys of toasted
marshmallows were new to her, but when she
tasted her first one she was prepared to agree
with Dolly that they were just the things to eat
in such a spot.

"I never liked them much before," said Bessie. "They're ever so much better when they're toasted this way."

"They're good for you, too," said Dolly, her mouth full of the soft confection. "At least, that's what everyone says, and I know they've never hurt me. Sometimes I eat so much candy that I don't feel well afterwards, but it's never been that way with toasted marshmallows. My, but I'm glad I found that box!"

"So'm I," admitted Bessie. "It seems to make the time pass to have them to eat. Here, let me toast some of them, now. You're doing all the work."

"I will not, you'd spoil them. It takes a lot of skill to toast marshmallows properly," Dolly boasted. "Heavens, Bessie, when there is something I can do well, let me do it. Aunt Mabel says she thinks I'd be a good cook if I would put my mind to it, but that's only because she likes the fudge I make."

"How do you make fudge?"

"Why, Bessie King! Do you mean to say you don't know? I thought you were such a good cook!"

"I never said so, Dolly. I had to do a lot of cooking at the farm when Maw Hoover wasn't well, but she never let me do anything but cook plain food. That's the only sort we ever had, anyhow. So I never got a chance to learn to make fudge or anything like that."

"Well, I'll teach you, when we get a good chance, Bessie," promised Dolly, seriously.

"I'll be glad to take lessons from you, Dolly," she said. "I think it would be fine to know how to make all sorts of candy. Then, if you did know, and could do it really well, you could make lots of it, and sell it. People always like candy, and in the city a lot of the shops have signs saying that they sell Home Made Candy and Fudge. So people must like it better than the sort they make in factories."

"I should say so, Bessie. But most of those stores are just cheating you, because the stuff they

3—C8

sell isn't home made at all. Everyone says mine
is much better.''

Bessie grew serious.

''Why, Dolly,'' she said, ''I think it would be
a fine idea to make candy to sell! I really believe
I'd like to do that—''

''I bet you would make just lots and lots of
money if you did,'' said Dolly, taking hold of a
new idea, as she always did, with enthusiasm.
''And we could get one of the stores to sell it for
us and keep some of the money for their trouble.
Suppose we sold it for fifty cents a pound, the
store would get twenty or twenty-five cents and
we'd get the rest. And—''

Bessie laughed.

''You're not forgetting that it costs something
to make, are you?'' she asked. ''You have to
allow for what it costs before you begin to think
of how you're going to spend your profits. But
I really do think it would work, Dolly. When we
get back to town we'll figure it all out, and see
how much it would cost for butter and sugar

and nuts and chocoate and all the things we'd
need.''

"Yes, and if we used lots of things we'd get
them cheaper, too, Bessie," said Dolly, surprising
Bessie by this exhibition of her business knowledge. "Oh, I think that would be fine. I'd just
love to have money that I'd earned myself. Some
of the other girls have been winning honor beads
by earning money, but I never could think of any
way that I could do it.''

Dolly was beginning to yawn, and Bessie herself felt sleepy. But when she proposed that they
should go into the tent now Dolly protested.

"Oh, let's stay outside, Bessie," she said. "If
we went in now we'd just wake ourselves up. We
can sleep out here just as well as not. What's
the difference?''

And Bessie was so sleepy that she was glad to
agree to that. In a few moments they were sound
asleep, with no thought of the exciting episodes
of the day and night to disturb them.

The fire was low when Bessie awoke with a

start. At first everything seemed all right; she could hear nothing. But then, suddenly, she looked over to where Dolly had been lying. There was no sign of her chum! And, just as Bessie herself was about to cry out, she heard a muffled call, in Dolly's tones, and then a loud crashing through the undergrowth near the camp, as someone or something made off swiftly through the woods! The gypsy had come back!

CHAPTER VIII

For a moment Bessie was too paralyzed with fear even to cry out. It was plain that the gypsy had carried poor Dolly away with him, and that, moreover, he had muffled her one cry for help. For a moment Bessie stood wondering what to do. To alarm the camp would be almost useless, she felt; the girls, waking up out of a sound sleep, could do nothing until they understood what had happened, and even then the chances were against their being able to help in any practical manner.

And so Bessie fought down that blind instinct to scream out her terror, and, in a moment, throwing off her blanket, she began to creep out into the black woods, dark now as pitch, and as impenetrable, it seemed, as one of the tropical jungles she had read of.

One thing Bessie felt to be, above everything,

117

necessary. She must find out what the gypsy meant to do, and where he was taking Dolly. If, by some lucky chance, she could track him, there would be a far better opportunity to rescue Dolly in the morning, when the guides would be called to help, and, if necessary, men from the hotel at Loon Pond and other places in the woods. To such a call for help, Bessie knew well there would be an instant response.

"He'll never go back to the camp," Bessie told herself, trying to argue the problem out, so that she might overlook none of the points that were involved, and that might make so much difference to poor Dolly, who was paying so dear a price for her prank. "If he did, he'd be sure that there would be people there, looking for him, as soon as the word got around that Dolly was missing."

She stopped for a moment, to listen attentively, but though the woods were full of slight noises, she heard nothing that she could decide positively was the gypsy. Still, burdened as he was with Dolly, it seemed to Bessie that he must make some

noise, no matter how skilled a woodsman he might
be, and how much training he had had in silent
traveling in his activities as a poacher and hunter
of game in woods where keepers were on guard.

"He'll find out some place where they're not
likely to look for him, and stay there until the
people around here have given up the idea of finding him," said Bessie to herself. "That's why
I've got to follow him now. And I'm sure he's
on one of the trails; he couldn't carry Dolly
through the thick woods, no one could. Oh, I
wish I could hear something!"

That wish, for the time, at least, was to be de-
nied, but it was not long before Bessie, still tramping through thick undergrowth in the direction
she was sure her quarry had taken, came to a
break in the woods, where it was a little lighter,
and she could see her way.

She saw at once that she had come to a trail,
and, though she had never seen it before, she
guessed that it was the one that led to Deer
Mountain, from what Miss Eleanor had told her

about the trails about the camp. And, moreover,
as she started to follow it, convinced that the
gypsy, on finding it, would have abandoned the
rougher traveling of the uncut woods, she saw
something that almost wrung a cry of startled
joy from her.

It was not much that she saw, only a fragment
of white cloth, caught in the branches of a bush
that had pushed itself out onto the trail. But
it was as good as a long letter, for the cloth was
from Dolly's dress, and it was plain and unmis-
takable evidence that her chum had been carried
along this trail.

She walked on more quickly now, pausing about
once in a hundred yards to listen for sounds of
those who were, as she was convinced, ahead of
her, and, about half a mile beyond the spot where
she had found that white pointer, she saw another
piece of mute but convincing evidence, of exactly
the same sort, and caught in the same way.

As Bessie kept on, the ground continued to rise,
and she realized that she must be on the crest

of Deer Mountain, one of the heights that lifted itself above the level of the surrounding woods. Although a high mountain, the climb from Long Lake was not a particularly severe one, for all the ground was so high that even the highest peaks in the range that was covered by these woods did not seem, unless one were looking at them from a distance of many miles, in the plain below, to be as high as they really were.

The trail that Bessie followed, as she knew, was leading her directly away from Loon Pond and the gypsy camp, but that did not disturb her, since she had expected the gypsy to bear away from his companions. Her mind was working quickly now, and she wondered just how far the gypsies were likely to go in support of their reckless companion.

She knew that the bonds among these nomads were very strong, but there was another element in this particular case that might, she thought, complicate matters. The man who had carried Dolly off was engaged to be married to the dark-eyed girl they had talked with, and it was possible that that fact might make trouble for him, and prevent him from receiving the aid of his tribe, as he would surely have done in any ordinary struggle with the laws of the people whom the gypsies seemed to despise and dislike.

Undoubtedly the girl's parents, if she had any, would resent the slight he was casting upon their daughter, and if they were powerful or influential in the tribe, they would probably try to get him cast out, and cause the other gypsies to refuse him the aid he was probably counting upon.

The most important thing, Bessie still felt, was to find out where Dolly was to be hidden. And, as she pressed on, tired, but determined not to give up what seemed to her to be the best chance of rescuing her chum, Bessie looked about constantly for some fresh evidence of Dolly's presence.

But luck was not to favor her again. Sharp as was her watch, there were no more torn pieces of Dolly's dress to guide her, and, even had Bessie

been an expert in woodcraft, and so able to follow their tracks, it was too dark to use that means
of tracing them.

Bessie did, indeed, think of that, and of waiting until some guide should come, who might be
able to read the message of the trail. But she
reflected that it was more than possible that none
of the men in the neighborhood might be able to
do so, and it seemed to her that it was better to
take the slim chance she had than abandon it in
favor of something that might, after all, turn out
to be no chance at all.

The darkness was beginning to yield now to
the first forerunners of the day. In the east there
was a faint radiance that told of the coming of
the sun, and Bessie hurried on, since she felt sure
that the gypsy would not venture to travel in daylight, and must mean to hide Dolly before the
coming of the sun lightened the task of his pursuers, since he must feel certain that he would
be pursued, although he might have no inkling
that anyone was already on his trail.

But now Bessie had to face a new problem that did, indeed, force her to rest. For suddenly the well defined, broad trail ended, and broke up into a series of smaller paths. Evidently this was a spot at which those who wished to reach the summit of the mountain took diverging paths, according to the particular spot they wanted to reach, and whether they were bound on a picnic or merely wanted to get to a spot whence they might see the splendid view for which Deer Mountain was famed.

In the darkness there was absolutely no way of telling which of these many diverging trails the gypsy had followed, and Bessie, ready to cry with disappointment and anxiety for Dolly, was forced to sit down on a stump and wait for daylight. Even that might not help her.

Her best chance, however, was to wait until the light came, and then, despite her lack of acquaintance with the art of reading footprints, to try to distinguish those of the gypsy. All that she needed was some clue to enable her to guess which path her quarry had taken; beyond that the message of the footprints was not necessary.

As she sat there, watching the slow, slow lightening in the east, Bessie wondered if the day was ever coming. She had seen the sun rise before, but never had it seemed so lazy, so inclined to linger in its couch of night.

But every wait comes to an end at last, and finally Bessie was able to go back a little way, before the other trails began to branch off, and bending over, to try to pick out the footprints of the man who had carried Dolly off. It was easy to do, fortunately, or Bessie could scarcely have hoped to accomplish it.

There had been a light rain the previous morning, enough to soften the ground and wipe out the traces of the numerous parties that had made Deer Mountain the objective point of a tramp in the woods, and, mingled with her own small footsteps, Bessie soon found the marks of hobnailed feet, that must, she was sure, have been made by the gypsy.

Step by step she followed them, and she **was** just about at the first of the diverging trails when a sound behind her made her turn, terrified, **to** see who was approaching.

But it was not the man who had so frightened her whom she saw as she turned. It was a girl— a gypsy, to be sure—but a girl, and Bessie had **no** fear of her, even when she saw that it was the same girl the scamp she was pursuing was **to** marry. Moreover, the girl seemed as surprised and frightened at the sight of Bessie, crouching there, as Bessie herself had been at the other's coming.

"Where is he; that wicked man you are **to** marry?" cried Bessie, fiercely, springing to her feet, and advancing upon the trembling gypsy girl. "You shall tell me, or I will—"

She seized the gypsy girl's shoulders, and shook her, before she realized that the girl, whose eyes were filled with tears, probably knew as little as she herself. Then, repentant, she released her shoulders, but repeated her question.

"You mean John, my man?" said the girl, a quiver in her tones. "I do not know, he was not at the camp last night. I was afraid. I think he does not love me any more."

Something about the way she spoke made Bessie pity her.

"What is your name?" she asked.

"Lolla," said the gypsy.

"I believe you do not know, Lolla," said Bessie, kindly. "And you do not want him to be sent to prison, perhaps for years and years, do you? You love this John?"

"Prison? They would send him there? What for? No, no—yes, I love him. Do you know where he is; where he was last night?"

"I know where he was last night, Lolla, yes. He came to our camp and carried my friend away. You remember, the one who was with me yesterday, when we looked at your camp? That is why I am looking for him. He says he will make her marry him later on; that he will keep her with your tribe until she is ready."

Lolla's tears ceased suddenly, and there was a gleam of passionate anger in her eyes.

"He will do that?" she said, angrily. "My brothers, they will kill him if he does that. He is to marry me, we are betrothed. You do not know where he is? You would like to find your friend?"

"I must, Lolla."

"Then I will help you, if you will help me. Will you?"

Lolla looked intently at Bessie, as if she were trying to tell from her eyes whether she really meant what she said.

"Oh, I wish I knew whether you are good; whether you speak the truth," cried the gypsy girl, passionately. "That other girl, your friend. She wants my John. So—"

Bessie, serious as the situation was, could not help laughing.

"Listen, Lolla," she said. "You mustn't think that. Dolly—that's my friend—thinks John is good looking, perhaps, but she hasn't even thought of marrying anyone yet, oh, for years and years. She's too young. We don't get married as early as you. So you may be sure that if John has her, all she wants is to get away and get back to her friends."

Lolla's eyes lighted with relief.

"That is good," she said. "Then I will help, for that is what I want, too. I do not want her to live in the tribe, and to be with us. You are sure John has taken her?"

Then Bessie told her of the face they had seen in the flashlight, and of how Dolly had been spirited away from the camp fire afterward. And as she spoke, she was surprised to see that Lolla's eyes shone, as if she were delighted by the recital.

"Why, Lolla, you look pleased!" said Bessie. "As if you were glad it had happened. How can that be; how can you seem as if you were happy about it?"

Lolla blushed slightly.

"He is my man," she said, simply. "He is strong and brave, do you not see? If he were not brave he would not dare to act so. He is a fine man. If I were bad, he would beat me. And he will beat anyone who is not good to me. Of course, I am glad that he was brave enough to act so, though I did not want him to do it.''

Bessie laughed. The primitive, elemental idea that was expressed in Lolla's words was beyond her comprehension, and, in fact, a good many people older and wiser than Bessie do not understand it.

But Lolla did not mind the laugh. She did not understand what was in Bessie's mind; what she had said seemed so simple to her that it required no explanation. And now her mind was bent entirely upon the problem of getting Dolly back to her friends, in order that John might turn back to her and forget the American girl whose appeal to him had lain chiefly in the fact that she was so different from the women of his own race.

''He will not take her back to camp,'' said Lolla, thoughtfully. ''He knows they would look there first.''

"But will the others—your people—help him?"

"He may tell them that he has stolen her to get a ransom; to keep her until her friends pay well for her to be returned. Our old men do not like that, they say it is too dangerous. But if he were to say that he had done so, they might help him, because our people stand and fall together. But," and her eyes shone, "I will tell my brothers the truth. They will believe me, and—Quick! Hide in those bushes; someone is coming!"

Bessie obeyed instantly. But, once she had hidden herself, she heard nothing. It was not for a minute or more after she had slipped into the bushes that she heard the sound that had disturbed Lolla. But then, looking out, she saw John coming down one of the paths, peering about him cautiously.

CHAPTER IX

AN UNEXPECTED ALLY

Bessie's heart leaped at the sight of the man who had given her her wild tramp through the night, and it was all she could do to resist her impulse to rush out, accuse him of the crime she knew he had committed, and demand that he give Dolly up to her at once. It was hard to believe that he was really dangerous.

Here, in the early morning light, his clothes soaked by the wet woods, as were Bessie's for that matter, he looked very cheap and tawdry, and not at all like a man to be feared. But a moment's reflection convinced Bessie that, for the time at least, it would be far wiser to leave matters in the hands of Lolla, the gypsy girl, who understood this man, and, if she feared him, and with cause, did so from reasons very different from Bessie's.

133

For a moment after he came in sight John did not see Lolla. Bessie watched the pair, so different from any people she had ever seen at close range before, narrowly. She was intensely interested in Lolla, and wondered mightily what the gypsy girl intended to do. But she did not have long to wait.

Lolla, with a little cry, rushed forward, and, casting herself on the ground at her lover's feet, seized his hand and kissed it. At first she said not a word; only looked up at him with her black, brilliant eyes, in which Bessie could see that a tear was glistening.

"Lolla! What are you doing here?"

At the sight of the girl John had started, nervously. It was plain that he did not feel secure; that he thought his pursuers might, even thus early, have tracked him down, and, in the moment before he had recognized Lolla, Bessie saw him quail, while his face whitened, so that Bessie knew he was afraid.

That knowledge, somehow, comforted her vast-

ly. It removed at once some of the formidable
quality which John had acquired in her eyes
when he stole Dolly after the fright that he must
have had when the flashlight powder exploded,
almost in his face. But Bessie remembered that
he had plucked up his courage after that scare;
the chances were that he would do so· again
now.

But, if Bessie was afraid of the kidnapper,
Lolla was not. She rose, and faced him defi-
antly. Bessie thought there was something splendid about the gypsy girl, and she wondered why
John, with such a girl ready and anxious to
marry him, had been diverted from her by Dolly,
charming though she was.

"I have come to save you, John," said Lolla.
"Where is the American girl you stole from her
friends?"

John started, evidently surprised by Lolla's
knowledge of what he had done, and said
something, sharply, in the gypsy tongue, which
Bessie, of course, could not understand. Her

question, it was plain, had fi ghtened, as well as
startled him; but it had also made him very
angry. Lolla, however, did not seem to mind
his anger. She faced him boldly, without giving ground, although he had moved toward
her with a threatening gesture of his uplifted
hand.

"Hit me, if you will," she said. "I am not
your wife yet, but when I am it will be your
right to strike me if you wish. But I know what
you have done. I know, too, that the Americans
know it. Do you think you can escape from these
woods without being caught?"

John stared at her angrily.

"I am going now to the camp," he said. "If
they come looking for news of the girl, they will
find me there, and plenty to swear that I have
been there all this night, and so could not have
done what they charge. My tribe will help me;
it is my right to call upon it for help."

"You forget me," said Lolla, dangerously. "I
will swear that I saw you here, where I came to

look for you because you had stayed away from the camp all the night. And when I tell my brothers, what will they swear?"

Again the man muttered something in the gypsy tongue, but under his breath. When he spoke aloud to Lolla it was in English.

"They are Barlomengri; they will support me. They will never let the policemen take me away. They are my brothers—"

"Do you think you can jilt their sister, the girl you asked for as your wife before all the tribe, and escape their vengeance? Do you think they will not punish you, even by seeing that you die in a prison, in a cell?"

And now John, beside himself with anger, fulfilled the threat of his uplifted hand, and struck Lolla sharply.

"Strike me again!" cried Lolla, furiously. "I have done no wrong! I am trying only to save you from your own folly. Tell me, at least, where you have hidden the girl? Would you have her starve? You will be watched, so that you may not bring her food. Had you thought of that?"

"Will you betray me? If you do not I shall not be watched. They will know as soon as they look for me that I was in the camp all through the night. Lolla, you fool, I love you, only you. I want her to win a ransom. They will pay to have her back, those Americans."

Lolla had guessed right when she had said that this would be his plea. But Bessie was surprised, and thought Lolla must also wonder at his telling her such a story. Lolla looked scornfully at John.

"I am no baby that I should believe such a tale as that," she said witheringly. "I give you your chance, John, your last chance. Will you take this girl back to her people, or set her free and show her the road? Or must I bear witness against you, and tell the tribe that you would shame me by forsaking me even before I am your wife?"

"Let me go," said John furiously. "We shall

see if a woman's talk is to be taken before mine.
You fool! Even your brothers will laugh at
your jealousy, and rejoice with me over the money
this girl will bring us. Let me pass—''

"Tell me, at least, where you have hidden her?
She will starve, I tell you—''

"She will not starve. Think you I know no
more than that of doing such a piece of work?
It is not the first time we have made anxious
fathers pay to win their children back! Ha-ha!
Peter, my friend, comes to take my watch. He
will see to it that she does not suffer for food.
And he will keep her safe for me. Out of my
way!''

He brushed Lolla aside roughly, and strode off
down the trail that Bessie had followed. For a
moment, while she could hear the sound of his
retreating footsteps, Lolla did not move. But
then she raised herself, a smile in her eyes, and
beckoned to Bessie.

"Go up that path, quickly,'' she whispered.
"Somewhere up there, hidden, you will find your

friend. Comfort her, but do not let her move.
If she is tied up, leave her so. Tell her that
help is near. I will free her.''

"But why—why not come with me, and free
her now?'' protested Bessie, eagerly. "We can
find her, for he came down that path, so he must
have left her somewhere up there. Oh, come,
Lolla, you will never regret it!''

"Did you not hear him say that Peter was coming? Peter is his best friend; they are closer
together, and are more to one another, than
brothers. If we tried to escape with her now,
Peter would find us, and his hand is heavy. We
should do your friend no good, and be punished
ourselves. We must wait. But hurry, before he
comes. Tell her to be happy, and not to fear. I
will save her, and you. We will work together
to save her.''

And with that Bessie, much as she would have
liked to get Dolly out of the clutches of her captor at once, had to be content. She realized fully
that in Lolla she had gained an utterly unex-

pected ally, in whom lay the best possible chance
for the immediate release of her chum, and the
mere knowledge of where Dolly was hidden would
be extremely valuable.

After all, it was all, and, possibly, more, than
she had expected to accomplish when she had
plunged into the woods after the gypsy and his
prisoner, and she felt that she ought to be satisfied. So she hurried at once up the path that
Lolla pointed out, leaving the gypsy girl below
as a guard.

The path was rough and steep, rising sharply,
but Bessie paid little heed to its difficulties, since
she felt that it was taking her to Dolly. She
kept her eyes and ears open for any sight or
sound that might make it easier to find Dolly,
but she did not call out, since she felt that it
was practically certain the gypsy had managed
in some manner, to make it impossible for poor
Dolly to cry out, lest, in his absence, she alarm
some passerby and so obtain her freedom.

Bessie was sure that Dolly would not be left

in some place that could be seen from the path, but she was also sure that she could not be far from it, since there had not been time for the gypsy to make any extended trip through the woods off the trail. Bessie had traveled fast through the night, and she was sure that John, with the weight of Dolly to carry, had not been able to move as fast as she, and could not, therefore, have been more than twenty minutes or half an hour ahead of her in reaching the trail she was now following.

So she watched carefully for some break in the thick undergrowth that lined the trail, for some opening through which John might have gone with his burden. There might even, she thought, be another of those precious sign posts that, back on the other trail, had been made by the torn pieces from Dolly's skirt.

But, careful as was her search, she reached the end of the trail without finding anything that looked like a promising place, or seeing anything that made her think Dolly was within a short dis-

tance of her. The trail led to an exposed peak, a
rugged outcrop of rock, bare of trees, and covered only with a slight undergrowth.

Once there Bessie understood why the trail had
been made through the woods. The view was
wonderful. Below her were the waving tops of
countless trees, and beyond them she could look
down and over the cultivated valleys, full of
farms, whose fields, marked off by stone fences,
looked small and insignificant from her high
perch.

Bessie, however, was in no mood to enjoy a
view. She wasted no time in admiring it, but
only peered over the edge of the peak on which
she stood, to satisfy herself that Dolly was not
hidden just below her. One look was enough to
do that. There was a way, she soon saw, of de-
scending, and reaching the woods again, but no
man, carrying any sort of a burden, could have
accomplished that descent.

It was a task that called for the use of feet
and hands and Bessie turned desperately, con-

vinced that she must, in some manner, have over-
looked the place at which John had turned off
the main trail with his burden.

Now, as she went downward, she searched the
woods at each side with redoubled care, and at
last she found what she had been looking for, or
what, it seemed to her, must be the place, since
she had seen no other that offered even a chance
for a successful passage through the thick growth
of trees and underbrush.

Without hesitation she turned off the trail, and,
though the going was rough, and her hands and
face were scratched, while her clothes were torn,
she was rewarded at last by finding that the
ground below her grew smooth, showing that
human feet had passed that way often enough to
wear the faintest sort of a path.

Once she became aware of the path her heart
grew light, for she was sure now that she was
going in the right direction at last. And, indeed,
it was not more than five minutes before she almost stumbled over Dolly herself, bound to a

tree, and with a handkerchief stuffed in her mouth so that she could not cry out.

"Oh, Dolly! I'm so glad, so glad! Listen, dear; I can't stay. You'll have to be here a little while longer, but we will soon have you back at the camp, as safe and well as ever. Are you hurt? Does it give you pain? If it doesn't shake your head sideways."

Dolly managed to shake her head, and in her eyes Bessie saw that now that she knew help was near Dolly's courage would sustain her.

"That gypsy girl we saw is near, but the man who carried you off is going to send another man to watch, and if I let you go now we'd only meet him, and be in more trouble than ever. But be brave, dear! it won't be long now."

Poor Dolly could not answer, for Bessie, remembering that Lolla had seemed to fear the man Peter more than she did John, dared not even loosen the gag. She saw, however, that while it must be making Dolly terribly uncomfortable, she could breathe, and that it was probably worse in appearance than in fact. So she leaned down and kissed her chum, and whispered in her ear.

"I'm going back to Lolla now, dear, but I'll soon be back with enough help so that we needn't care how many of the gypsies there are near us. If I stay now I'm afraid they'll catch me, too, and then no one would know where you were. They can't get you away from here, so you're sure to be safe soon."

Dolly nodded to show that she understood, and Bessie moved silently away. But, as she turned down the trail that would take her back to the spot where she had left Lolla, she had a new cause for fright. She heard Lolla's voice, raised loudly, arguing with a man who answered in low, guttural tones. What they were saying she could not distiguish, but somehow she understood that Peter had come even sooner than Lolla had feared, and the gypsy girl, at the risk of angering him, was trying to warn her, so that she might not descend the trail and so stumble right into his arms.

So, although the prospect frightened her, she turned and made her way swiftly up to the peak again, determined that if the man should go past the opening that led to the place where Dolly lay, she would risk the danger and the difficulty of the rocky descent from the peak itself.

As she hastened along silence fell behind her, and she knew that Peter must have started. He was whistling a queer gypsy tune and Bessie heard him pass the partly masked opening that she had herself found with so much difficulty.

After that she hesitated no longer, but rushed to the rocky top of the peak, and in a moment she was making her way down, with as much caution as possible, swinging from one ledge to the next, hanging on to a bush here, and a projecting piece of rock there.

Even an expert climber, equipped with rope and sharp pointed stick, would have found the descent difficult. And all that enabled Bessie to succeed was her knowledge that she must.

CHAPTER X

A TERRIBLE SURPRISE

Bessie, though she had to pause more than once in her wild descent of the rocks, dared not look back to see if the gypsy, Peter, was pursuing her, or even whether he was looking down after her. She had two reasons. For one thing, the task was difficult and terrifying enough as it was, and to know that there was danger from behind, as well as the peril involved in the descent itself, would, she feared, unnerve her.

And, moreover, even if Peter saw her, he might not, if she paid no attention to him, suspect that she had anything to do with Dolly, or that he and his companion had anything to dread from her. Bessie did not know whether he would recognize her as having been at the gypsy camp with Dolly, but she felt that it would be as well not to take the chance. Things were bad enough without running the risk of complicating them still further.

The descent was a long and hard one, but when she was about half way down to the comparatively level ground at the foot of the peak, all real danger of a crippling fall was over, since there a path began. Evidently some trampers who were fond of climbing had worn it through the rough surface to a point where a good view was to be had, and had stopped there, content with the distance they had gone, and not disposed to try the further ascent. And as soon as Bessie reached that point she was able to stop and get her breath.

Meanwhile she wondered what had become of Lolla. The gypsy girl, as Bessie understood thorougly, was running severe risks. If the two men knew that she was in league with Dolly's friends they would certainly take some steps to silence her. But John, Bessie felt sure, did not believe that Lolla, no matter how jealous she might be, would actually betray her own people to the hated

Americans. He had smiled in a confident manner while Lolla had made her threats, and Bessie
thought he regarded the girl as a child in a temper, but sure to come to her senses before she
actually put him in danger.

What to do next was a problem. Bessie, when
she had followed the rough path until it led to
a trail, was completely lost. She knew, roughly,
and in a general way, the direction of Camp
Manasquan, as the camp at Long Lake was called,
but that was about all.

"If I go straight ahead I may be going just as
straight as I can away from anyone who can
help Dolly," she reflected. "Or I may get over
toward Loon Pond, and run into that awful gypsy,
and then I'd be worse off than ever! Oh, I do
wish I knew where I was, or how I can find Lolla.
She must know these woods, and she'd be able
to help me, I'm sure."

Finally, however, Bessie determined to move
slowly along the trail in a direction that would,
she thought, take her around the bottom of Deer

Mountain. She remembered that just a little while before she had come to the place where she had first seen Lolla, a side path had crossed the trail on which she had followed Dolly and her captor, and it seemed likely to her that that path would also cross the trail she was now on.

If it did she could work back to a spot she knew, and so find her bearings, at least. Then, if there was nothing else to be done, she would certainly be able to get back to Long Lake. For her to stay in the woods, lost and hungry, would not help Dolly.

So she set out bravely, walking as fast as she could. The sun was high in the heavens now, and it was long after breakfast time, so that Bessie was hungry, but she thought little of that.

As she had hoped, and half expected, she came, presently, and at what seemed to her the proper place, upon a trail that crossed the one she was following, and she turned to the left without hesitation. She might, she felt, be going in the wrong direction altogether, but she could not very well be more hopelessly lost than she was already, and, if she had to be out in the woods without a clue to the proper way to turn, she felt that it made very little difference whether she was in one place or in another.

The new trail was one evidently little used, and when Bessie had been on it for perhaps ten minutes, and was beginning to think that it was time she came in sight of the larger trail from Long Lake to Deer Mountain, she heard someone coming toward her, and, rounding a bend, came into sight of Lolla.

The gypsy girl seemed overwhelmed with joy at the sight of Bessie.

"Oh, how glad I am!" she exclaimed. "I was afraid that Peter had caught you and tied you up with your friend, and that you would think I had sent you up there so that he would trap you! How did you escape?"

"I climbed down the rocks," said Bessie simply, and smiled at Lolla's gasp of astonishment.

"*You* climbed down the rocks!" cried the

gypsy. "However did you do that? There ain't many men—not even many of our men—would try that, I can tell you. I thought perhaps you would try to do that, and I was coming around this way to get to the foot of the rocks and see if I could find out what had become of you."

"You know where we are and how to get back, then?" asked Bessie.

"Of course I do. I know all these woods." Lolla laughed. "I have set traps for partridges and rabbits here many and many a time, but the guides never saw me. You knew where you were going, didn't you? If you'd kept on as you were going when you met me you would have come to the main trail in a minute or two, and then, if you'd turned to the right, and kept straight on, you'd have come to Long Lake, where you started from."

"I thought that was what would happen, Lolla, but I wasn't quite sure."

"Did you hear me shouting when Peter came

along? I hoped you would understand and hide yourself some way, so that he wouldn't find you. What I was most afraid of was that you would be in the woods with your friend, and that you wouldn't hear us.''

''Yes, I heard you, and I knew what you were doing, Lolla; that you meant to warn me that Peter had come sooner than you thought he would. I was grateful, too, but I was afraid just to hide myself and let him go by, because the woods were so thick on each side of the trail that I was afraid he would see where I had broken through and catch me.''

Lolla nodded her head.

''You are wise. You would be a good gypsy, Bessie. You would soon learn all the things we know ourselves. Peter has very quick eyes, and he is very suspicious, too. He saw you at the camp, you know, and he would have guessed right away, if he had seen you there, that you were looking for Dolly.''

''That was just what I was afraid of, Lolla.

He would have tied me up with her if he had found me, wouldn't he?''

"Yes. He's a bad man, that Peter. I think if John and he were not so friendly John would not have done this. He is kind, and brave, and he always tried to stop anyone who wanted to steal children. He would steal a horse, or a deer, but never a child; that was cowardly, he said.''

"He didn't hurt you, did he, Lolla?''

The gypsy girl laughed.

"Oh, no. He tried to hit me, but I got away from him too quickly. I would not let him touch me. With John it is different. He is my man; he may beat me if he likes. But not Peter; I hate him. If he beat me I would put this into him.''

Bessie, surprised by the look of hate in Lolla's eyes, drew back in fear as Lolla produced a long, sharp knife from the folds of her dress, and flourished it for a moment.

"Oh, Lolla, please put that away!'' she exclaimed. "There's no one here to be afraid of.''

Lolla laughed.

"No, but I have it if I need it," she said mean-
ingly.

"What are we going to do now, Lolla? We
can't leave Dolly up there much longer. They've
got her tied up, and gagged, so that she can't
call out, and she's terribly uncomfortable, though
I don't think she's suffering much."

"We will get her soon," said Lolla, confidently.

"You stay near where she is, so that they can't
get her away," said Bessie, "and I'll go and get
help. Then we shan't have any trouble."

But Lolla frowned at the suggestion.

"You would get those guides, and they would
catch my man and put him in prison, oh, for
years, perhaps! No, no; I will get her away,
with you to help me. Leave that to me. Peter is
stupid. Come with me now; I know what we
must do."

"Where are you going? This isn't the way
back to where Dolly is," protested Bessie, as
Lolla pressed on in the direction from which

Bessie had come. "We can never get up those rocks, Lolla; it was hard enough to come down."

"We are not going there, not yet," said Lolla. "I must go to the camp and find out what John is doing. If he comes back to watch her himself it will be harder. But if he has to stay, and Peter looks after her, then we shall have no trouble. You shall see; only trust me. I managed so that you saw her, didn't I? Doesn't that show you that I can do what I say?"

"I suppose so," sighed Bessie. "I should think you wouldn't care if that man does go to prison, though, Lolla. He isn't nice to you, and you say he'll beat you when you're married. American men don't beat their wives. If they did they would be sent to prison. I should think you'd give him up—"

Lolla's dark eyes flamed for a moment, but then she smiled, as if she had remembered that Bessie, not being a gypsy, could not be expected to understand the gypsy ways.

"He is a good man," she said. "He will al-

ways see that I have enough to eat, and pretty
things to wear. And if he beats me, it will be
because I have been wicked, and deserve to be
beaten. When I am his wife he will be like my
father; if I am bad he will punish me. Is it not
so among your people?''

Bessie struggled with a laugh at the thought
of the only married couple she had ever known
at all well: Paw and Maw Hoover. The idea that
Paw Hoover, the mildest and most inoffensive of
men, might ever beat his wife would have made
anyone who knew that couple laugh.

Instead of turning when they reached the trail
which Bessie had followed after her descent from
the rocks, Lolla led the way straight on.

''Are you sure you know where you are going,
Lolla?'' asked Bessie.

Lolla smiled at her scornfully.

''Yes, but it is not the way you would go,''
she said. ''The trail to the camp will be full
of people. They will be out all over the camp
particularly. We must come to it from another

direction. That is why we are going this way.''

It was not long before Bessie was as thoroughly lost as if she had been in a maze. Lolla, however, seemed to know just where she was going. She left one trail to turn into another without ever showing the slightest doubt of her direction, and, at times, when the woods were thin, she would take short cuts, leading the way through entirely pathless portions of the forest with as much assurance as if she had been walking through the streets of a city where she had lived all her life. Even Bessie, used to long walks around Hedgeville, in which she had learned the country thoroughly, was surprised.

''I don't believe I'd ever get to know these woods as well as you do,'' she said admiringly. ''Why, you never seem even to hesitate.''

''I've been here every summer since I was born,'' said Lolla, in a laughing tone. ''I ought to know these woods pretty well, I think.''

''I hope no one sees us now,'' said Bessie, nervously. "I really do feel as if it were wrong for me to keep away. Miss Mercer must be as anxious about me as she is about Dolly."

"Is she the lady who is with you girls?"

"Yes. You see, she probably thinks that I was carried off, as well as Dolly."

"She will stop being anxious all the sooner for not knowing where you are. I think it will not be long now before we get your friend away from that place where she is hidden."

"Well, I certainly hope so. Listen! I think I can hear voices in front of us."

"I heard them two or three minutes ago," said Lolla, with a smile. "Stay here, now; hide behind that clump of bushes. I will go ahead and see what I can find. Even if it is some of your friends they would not suspect me; they would think I was just out for a walk."

So Bessie waited for perhaps ten minutes, while Lolla crept forward alone. But the gypsy was back soon, smiling.

"All is safe now," she said. "Come quickly,

3—C14

though, so we shall get behind them and be able
to get near the camp. There is a place there
where you may hide while I find out what is
going on.''

They reached the spot Lolla meant in a few
minutes more, and again Bessie had to play the
inactive part and wait while Lolla went on to
gain the information she needed. When she came
back she was smiling happily.

''That John is stupid, though he is so brave,''
she said to Bessie. ''He went back there to the
camp, and he is sitting in front of his wagon.
There is a guide with a gun sitting near him,
and my sister tells me that the guide says he
will follow him and shoot him if he tries to get
away.

''There are many people there, and the whole
camp is angry and frightened. The king says he
will punish John, but John will not admit that
he knows where your friend is. We are safe
from him. They will not let him get away for
a long time.''

Bessie was comforted by the news. With her captor under guard, Dolly had nothing to fear from him, and, though Peter might be a sullen and a dangerous man, Bessie felt that Lolla was right, and that he was too thick witted to be greatly feared.

They made the return trip with hearts far lighter than they had been as they made their way to the gypsy camp. Bessie had seen that Lolla was afraid of John, though now that he had been over-reached she was ready enough to laugh at him.

"What are you going to do? How are you going to get her away, Lolla?" asked Bessie, as they neared the point where she had first seen her ally.

"I don't know yet," said Lolla, frankly. "If Peter is on the trail it will be harder. I hope he will be inside, so that we can slip by without his seeing us. If he is, and we get by, then you are to wait until you hear me sing. So."

She sang a bar or two of a gypsy melody, and

repeated it until Bessie, too, could hum it, to prove that she had it right, and would not fail to recognize it.

"When you hear me sing that, remember that you n ast run down and go to your friend. Here is my knife. Use it to cut the cords that tie her. Then you and she must go back toward the rocks where you went down. And when you hear me sing again you are to go down, as quickly as you can, but quietly, and, as soon as you are past the place where she was hidden, you must start running. I will try to catch up with you and go with you, but do not wait for me."

"I don't quite understand," Bessie began.

But now Lolla was the general, brooking no defiance. She stamped her foot.

"It does not matter whether you understand or not," she said sharply. "If you want me to save your friend and get back to the others you must do as you are told, and quickly. Now, come."

They went on up the trail, and, at the bend just below the spot where she had broken through to reach Dolly before, Bessie waited while Lolla, who had recognized the place from Bessie's description of it, crept forward to make sure that the way was clear.

"All right," she whispered. "Come on."

Silently, but as swiftly as they could, they crept past the place, and, when they were out of sight, stopped.

"Now, you will know my song when you hear it?"

"Yes, indeed, Lolla. Why, what have you got there?"

"What I need to make Peter come with me," laughed Lolla. "See, a fine meal, is it not? I got it at the camp. Let him smell that stew and he would follow me out of the woods."

Bessie began to understand Lolla's plan at last. She was going to tempt Peter to betray his orders from his friend by appealing to his stomach. And Bessie wondered again, as she had many

times since she had met Lolla, at the cunning of
the gypsy girl.

Her confidence in Lolla was complete by now,
and she did not at all mind waiting as she saw
the little brightly clad figure disappear amidst
the green of the trail.

It was some time, however, before she heard
any signs that indicated that Lolla had obtained
any results. And then it was not the song she
heard, but Lolla's clear laugh, rising above the
heavy tones of Peter.

"Oh, oh! You would give me orders when I
bring you breakfast? No, no, Peter; that won't
do. Come, she is safe there; come and eat with
me, where she cannot put a spell on your food
to make it choke you."

"Do you think she would do that?"

That was Peter's voice, stupid and filled with
doubt. Bessie laughed at Lolla's cleverness.
Peter, she thought, would be just the sort of
man to yield to the fears of superstition.

"I know she would; she hates us. Come, Peter;
does it not look good?"

"Give it to me. There, I'll catch you—"

Then there was a sound of scuffling and running, but Bessie, noticing that it drew further
and further away, laughed. Lolla was a real
strategist. She understood how to handle the big
gypsy, evidently. And a moment later Bessie, her
nerves quivering, all alert as she waited for the
signal, heard the notes of Lolla's song. At once
she rushed down, broke through the tangled
growth, and was at Dolly's side, cutting away at
the cords that bound Dolly, and, first of all, tear-
ing the handkerchief from her mouth.

"It's all right now, we're safe, Dolly. Only
you'll have to come quickly, dear, when I get you
free. There, that's it. Are you stiff? Can you
stand up?"

"I guess so," gasped Dolly. "Oh, I'd do anything to get away from here. Bessie, look!"

Bessie turned, to face Peter and Lolla, their
faces twisted into malignant grins. Lolla had
betrayed her!

CHAPTER XI

For a moment Bessie stared at the two gypsies, their eyes glowing with malicious triumph
and delight at her shocked face, in such dazed
astonishment that she could not speak at all. She
had been completely outwitted and hoodwinked.
She had trusted Lolla utterly; had made up her
mind that the girl's jealousy was not feigned.

Even now, for a wild moment, the thought
flashed through her mind that perhaps Lolla had
been unable to help herself; that Peter might
have insisted on coming back, and that Lolla was
forced, in order to be of help later on, to seem
to fall in with his plans.

But Lolla herself soon robbed her of the comfort that lay in such a thought.

"You thought I would betray my people!" she
cried, shrilly. "We do not do that; no, no! Ah,

169

but it was easy to deceive you! When I saw you
I knew you would be dangerous. I could not
hold you by force until John came, I had to trick
you. I thought we would catch you when you
went up there. I did not think you would be
brave enough to go down the rocks.''

Bessie said not a word, but only clung to Dolly's
hand and stared at the treacherous gypsy.

"So then, when you had gone, I had to find
you again, and send word to Peter to do as I
said, so that we could catch you, and stop you
from going to your friends and telling them
where we had hidden your friend who is there
with you now. Now we have two, instead of one.
Oh, I have done well, have I not, Peter?''

Peter grinned, and grunted something in his
own tongue that made Lolla smile.

"Tie them up again, Peter,'' said Lolla, looking viciously at Bessie, and obviously gloating
over the way in which she had tricked the American girl. And Peter, nothing loath, advanced to
do so. But Bessie had stood all she could.

Dolly, terribly cast down by this sudden up-
setting of all the hopes of rescue that the coming
of Bessie and her release from the cords that
bound her had raised, was close beside her, shiv-
ering with fright and despair.

And Bessie, with a sudden cry of anger, seized
the knife Lolla had given her, which had been
lying at her feet. Furiously she brandished it.

"If either of you come a step nearer I'll use
it!" she said, scarcely able to recognize her own
voice, so changed was it by the anger that Lolla's
treachery had aroused in her. "You'd better not
think I'm joking. I mean it!"

Peter hesitated, but Lolla, her eyes flashing,
urged him on.

"Go on! Do you want me to tell all the women
that you were frightened by a little girl; a girl
you could crush with one hand?" she cried,
angrily. "You coward! Tie them up, I tell you!
Oh, if my man John were here he'd show you!
Here—"

Peter, stung by her taunts, made a quick rush

forward. For a moment Bessie did not know
what to do. She wondered if, when it came to
the test, she would really be able to use the knife;
to try to cut or stab this man. He was getting
nearer each moment, and, just as she was almost
within his grasp she darted back and aimed a
blow at him with the knife.

There was no danger that it would strike him;
Bessie thought that, if she could only convince
him that she had meant what she said, he would
hesitate. And she was right. He gave a cry of
alarm as he saw the steel flash toward him and
drew back.

"She would stab me!" he exclaimed furiously,
to Lolla. "I was not to be struck with a knife.
John said nothing about that. He told me only
to guard this girl—"

"She wouldn't really touch you with it,"
screamed Lolla, so furious that she forgot the
need of keeping her voice low. "John wouldn't
let her frighten him that way, he is too brave.
Oh, how the women will laugh when they hear

how the brave Peter was frightened by a girl with
a little knife!"

But Bessie, in spite of her own indecision, had
managed, somehow, to convince the man that she
was serious, and Lolla's taunts no longer affected
him. He drew back still further, and stood looking stupidly at the two girls.

"You're wiser than she," said Bessie approv-
ingly. "I meant just what I said. Keep as far
as that from me, and you'll be safe. I'm not
afraid of you any more."

Nor was she. Her victory, brief though it
might be, had encouraged her, and revived her
drooping spirits. Dolly, too, seemed to have
gained new life from the sight of the big gypsy
quailing before her chum. She had stopped
trembling, and stood up bravely now, ready to
face whatever might come.

"Good for you, Bessie!" she exclaimed. She
darted a vicious look at Lolla. "I wish that
treacherous little gypsy would come somewhere
near me," she went on, angrily. "I'd pull her

hair and make her sorry she ever tried to help
those villains to keep us. When they put her
in prison I'm going to see her, and jeer at
her!''

Lolla, looking helpless now in her anger, said
nothing, but she glared at the two girls.

''I think these people are very superstitious,''
whispered Dolly to Bessie, when it became plain
that, for the moment, the two gypsies intended
only to watch them, without making any further
attempt to tie them up.

''I think so too,'' returned Bessie, in the same
tone. ''But I don't see what good that is going
to do us, Dolly.''

''Neither do I, just yet, Bessie. But I can't
help thinking that there must be some way that
we could frighten them, if we could only think
of it; so that they would be frightened and run
away.''

''We might tell them—Oh, I've got an idea,
Dolly.''

She looked at Peter and Lolla. They were at

the very edge of the little clearing in which Dolly
had been imprisoned.

"Listen, Lolla," said Bessie, calmly. "I believe that you are a good girl, though you have
lied to me, and tried to make me think you were
my friend, when all the time you were planning
how you could betray me. This place is dangerous."

Lolla looked at her scornfully and tossed her
head.

"Don't think you can frighten me with your
stories," she said, with a laugh. "It is dangerous
—for you. When my man comes you will find
that he is not a coward, like Peter, to be frightened with your knife. He will take it away from
you and beat you, too, for trying to frighten
Peter with it."

"Yes, he is brave, Lolla. We saw that when
he ran away from the fire that he saw last night
near the lake."

Bessie was taking a chance when she said that.
She did not know whether Lolla had heard of the

mysterious flashlight explosion or not, but she
thought it more than probable that John had told
her of it. And she was reasonably sure that he
was still wondering what had caused the light
that had so suddenly blinded him. Her swift look
at Lolla showed her that her blow had struck
home.

"He is a brave man, indeed, to keep on with
his wicked plan to steal my friend after such a
warning," Bessie went on sternly. "But his
bravery will do him no good. There is a spirit
looking after us. It made the fire that frightened him, and the next time he will not only see
the fire; he will feel it, too."

Now she looked not only at Lolla, who seemed
shaken, but at Peter, who was staring at her as
if fascinated. Evidently he, too, had heard of
the strange fire. Bessie had reckoned on the
probability, that seemed almost a certainty, that
John would not have been able to explain, even
to himself, the nature of the flashlight explosion.
And evidently she was right. Then she took an-

other chance, guessing at what she thought John would probably have said to explain the fire.

"I know what he told you," she said slowly. "He said that the fire came from a spirit that was guiding him, and was trying to help him. But he only said that because he did not understand. It meant just the opposite; that it would be better for him to go home, and forget the wicked plot he had thought of."

Peter seemed to be weakening, but Lolla tossed her head again.

"Are you a baby? Do you think that is true?" she said to him. "Don't you see that she is only trying to frighten you, as she did with the knife?"

"Indeed I am not," said Bessie, earnestly. "I am not angry with you, any more than I am afraid of you now. If you stay here something dreadful will happen to you both. You would not like to go to prison, would you, and stay there all through this summer, and the next winter, and the summer of next year, when you might be traveling the road with your brothers?"

3—C12

"Make them keep quiet, Peter," cried Lolla,
furiously. "She is quite right. There is danger
here, but it comes from her friends. She thinks
that if she can fool us into letting her talk, they
may pass by and hear her voice."

"You keep quiet," said Peter, doggedly, evidently deciding that, this time, he could safely
obey Lolla's orders, and quite ready to do so.
"If you make any more noise I will—"

He left the sentence uncompleted, but a savage
gesture showed what he meant. He had a stout
stick, and this he now swung with a threatening
air.

Bessie had hoped to work on the superstitious
nature of the gypsy man, and to frighten him,
perhaps, if she had good luck, into letting her
go off with Dolly. But Lolla's interference had
put that out of the question. She turned sadly
to Dolly, to see her companion's eyes twinkling.

"Never you mind, Bessie," she said. "They're
stupid, anyhow. And as long as they don't tie
us up we're all right. I'd just as soon be here

as anywhere. Someone will go along that trail presently looking for us, and when they do we can shout. They'll probably make a noise themselves, so as to let us know they are near. And I'm not frightened any more; really I'm not."

But Bessie, tired and disappointed, was nearer to giving in than she had been since the moment when she had awakened and found that Dolly was missing. She felt that she ought to have distrusted Lolla; that she had made a great mistake in thinking, even for a moment, that the gypsy girl meant to betray her own people.

Then suddenly a strange thing happened. A new voice, that belonged to none of the four who were in the clearing, suddenly broke the silence. It seemed to come from a tree directly over the heads of Lolla and Peter, and, as it spoke, they stared upward with one accord, listening intently to what it said.

"Will you make me come down and punish you?" said the voice. It was that of an old, old man, feeble with age, but still clear.

Bessie stared too, as surprised as the gypsy, and the voice went on:

"I gave your companion a sign last night that should have warned him. I speak to you now, to warn you again. The next time I shall not give a warning; I shall act, and your punishment will be swift and terrible. Take heed; go, while there is time."

For a moment the two gypsies were speechless, looking at one another in wonder, and Bessie was not disposed to blame them. Her own head was in a whirl.

"Quick; it is in that tree!" said Lolla, easily the braver of the two of them. "Climb up there, and see who it is that is trying to frighten us, Peter."

But Peter was not prepared to do anything of the sort. He was trembling, and casting nervous glances behind him, as if he were more minded to make a break and run down the trail.

"Climb yourself! I shall stay here," he retorted.

And Lolla, without further hesitation, sprang into the branches of the tree and began to climb.

As she did so the mysterious voice sounded again.

"You cannot see me, yet," it said. "You can only hear me. See, my voice is in your ears, but you cannot see as much as my little finger. Beware; go before you *do* see me. For when you do, you will regret it; regret it as long as you live!"

When Lolla, a moment later, reached firm ground again, she was trembling, and Bessie saw that her courage was beginning to fail. She looked about her nervously, as Peter was doing. And suddenly the voice spoke again, but this time it shouted, and it was in a stronger, more vigorous tone, and one of great anger.

"Must I show myself? Must I punish you?" it said, furiously. "Fear me; you will do well! Go—GO!"

With a yell of terror Peter turned suddenly, and ran through the thick bushes toward the trail, crying out as he went, and stumbling.

"Come; it is the devil! I saw his horns and his tail then," he screamed. "Come, Lolla, this is an accursed place. I told John it was wrong to try to do this; that he would get into trouble."

"He is wise; he is safe!" said the mysterious voice. "Go too, Lolla; I am growing impatient. Go, if you want to see John, your lover, and the brothers that you love, again. The time is growing short. I come; I come; and when I come—"

And then at last Lolla's nerves, too, gave way, and she followed Peter, screaming, as he had done, while she ran. Bessie, as astonished and almost as frightened as the two gypsies had been, turned then to see how Dolly was bearing this extraordinary affair, to see her chum rolling about on the ground, with tears in her eyes.

"Oh, that was funny!" Dolly exclaimed. "They were easy, after all, Bessie."

"They've gone! It's all right now," said Bessie. "But who was it, Dolly? Who could it have been?"

"It was me!" exclaimed Dolly, weakly, between gasps of laughter, forgetting her grammar altogether. "I learned that trick last summer. They call it ventriloquism. It just means throwing your voice out so that it doesn't seem to come from you at all, and changing it, so that people won't recognize it."

Bessie stared at her, in wonder and admiration.

"Why, Dolly Ransom!" she said. "However do you do it? I never heard of such a thing!"

"I don't know how I do it," said Dolly, recovering her breath. "No one who can does, I guess. It's just something you happen to be able to do."

"You certainly frightened them," said Bessie. "And you saved us with your trick, Dolly. I think they've run clear away. We can follow them down the trail; they won't stick to it, and I think we can go right back to Long Lake, now, without being afraid any more. Come on, we'd better start. I don't want to stay here."

CHAPTER XII

OUT OF THE FRYING PAN

"Stay here? I should say not!" exclaimed Dolly. "I'm almost starved—and, Bessie, they must be terribly worried about us, too. And now tell me, as we go along, how you ever found me. I don't see how you managed that."

So, as they made their way down the trail, Bessie told her of all that had happened since her rude awakening at the camp fire, just after the gypsy had carried Dolly off.

"Oh, Bessie, it was perfectly fine of you, and it's only because of you that we're safe now! But you oughtn't to have taken such a risk! Just think of what might have happened!"

"That's just it, Dolly. I've got time to think about it now, but then I could only think of you, and what was happening to you. If I'd stopped to think about the danger I'm afraid I wouldn't have come."

"But you must have known it was dangerous! I don't know anyone else who would have done it for me."

"Oh, yes, they would, Dolly. That's one of the things we promise when we join the Camp Fire Girls—always to help another member of the Camp Fire who is in trouble or in danger."

"Yes—but not like that. It doesn't say anything about going into danger yourself, you know."

"Listen, Dolly. If you saw me drowning in the water, you'd jump in after me, wouldn't you? Or after any of the girls—if there wasn't time to get help?"

"I suppose so—but that's different. It just means going in quickly, without time to think very much about it. And you had plenty of time to think while you were tramping along that horrid dark trail after me."

"Well, it's all over now, Dolly, and, after all, you had to save both of us in the end."

"That was just a piece of luck, and a trick,

Bessie. It didn't take any courage to do that—and, beside, if it hadn't been for you I would never have had the chance to do that. I wonder why Lolla let you have her knife to cut those cords about me?''

"I think she's a regular actress, Dolly, and that she wanted to make me feel absolutely sure she was on our side, so that we would both be there in that trap when she and Peter came back.''

"It's a good thing he was such a coward, Bessie.''

"Oh, I think he'd be brave enough if he just had to fight with a man, so that it was the sort of fighting he was used to. You see it wasn't his plan, and when I said I'd use that knife he couldn't see why he should run any risk when all the profit was for the other man.''

"And when you played that trick with your voice he was frightened, because he'd never heard of anything of that sort, and he didn't know what was coming next. I think that would frighten a good many people who are really brave.''

"Bessie, why do I always get into so much trouble? All this happened just because I changed those signs that day."

"Oh, I don't know about that, Dolly. It might have happened anyhow. I've got an idea now that they knew we were around, and that John planned to kidnap one of us and keep us until someone paid him a lot of money to let us go. Something Lolla said made me think that."

"Then he was just playing a joke when he said he wanted to marry me?"

"Yes, I think so, because I don't think he was foolish enough to think he could ever really get you to do that. I did think so at first, but if that had been so I'm quite sure that Lolla wouldn't have helped him."

"She'd have been jealous, you mean?"

"Yes, I'm quite sure, you see, that she saw him and talked to him when we went over to their camp that time, so that she could take orders from him to Peter. He knew he'd be

watched, so he must have made up his mind
from the first that he would have to have
help.''

"I wonder what he is doing now, Bessie.''

"I certainly hope he's still over there at the
camp, sitting near that guide. The guide said
he would shoot him if he tried to get away, you
know.''

"My, but I'll bet there's been a lot of commo-
tion over this.''

"I'm sure there has, Dolly. Probably all the
people at the hotel heard about it, too. I'll bet
they've got people out all through the woods
looking for us.''

"I wish we'd meet some of them—and that
they'd have a lot of sandwiches and things. Bessie, I've simply got to sit down and rest. I want
to get back to Miss Eleanor and the girls, but
if I keep on any longer I'll drop just where we
are. I'm too tired to take another step without
a rest.''

"I am, too, Dolly. Here—here's a good place

to sit down for a little while. We really can't be
so very far from Long Lake now."

"No," said a voice, behind them. "But you're
so far that you'll never reach there, my dears!"

And, turning, they saw John, the gypsy, leering
at them. His clothes were torn, and he was hot
and dirty, so that it was plain that he had had
a long run, and a narrow escape from capture.
But at the sight of them he smiled, evilly and
triumphantly, as if that repaid him amply for
any hardships he had undergone.

"Don't you dare touch us!" said Bessie, shrilly,

She realized even as she said it, that he was
not likely to pay any attention to her, but the
sight of his grinning face, when she had been so
sure that their troubles were over at last, was
too much for her.

She sank down on a log beside Dolly, and hid
her face in her hands, beginning to cry. Most
men, no matter how bad, would have been moved
to pity by the sight of her sufferings. But John
was not.

"Don't cry," he said, with mock sympathy. "I am not going to treat you badly. You shall stay in the woods with me. I have a good hiding place, a place where your friends will never find you until I am ready. You are tired. So am I. We will rest here. It is quite safe. A party of your friends passed this way five minutes ago. They will not come again—not soon. I was within a few feet of them, but they did not see me."

Bessie groaned at the news. Had they only reached the place five minutes earlier, then, they would have been safe. She was struck by an idea, however, and lifted her voice in a shout for aid. In a moment the gypsy's hand covered her mouth and he was snarling in her ear.

"None of that," he said, grittingly, "or I will find a way to make you keep still. You must do as I tell you now, or it will be the worse for you. Will you promise to keep quiet?"

Bessie realized that there was no telling what this man would do if she did not promise—and keep her promise. He was cleverer than Peter, and, therefore, much more dangerous. She felt, somehow, that the trick which had worked so well when Dolly had used it before would be of no avail now. He might even understand it; he was most unlikely, she was sure, to yield to super- stitious terror as Peter and Lolla had done. And, leaning over to Dolly, she whispered to her.

"Don't try that trick, Dolly. You see, if the others had dared the voice to do something they would have found out that there was really noth- ing to be afraid of—and I'm afraid he'd wait. It may be useful again, but not with him, now. If we tried it, and it didn't work—"

"I understand," Dolly whispered back. "I think you are right, too, Bessie. We'd be worse off than ever. I was thinking that if only some of the other gypsies were here we might frighten them so much with it that they'd make him let us go."

"Yes. We'll save it for that."

The gypsy was still breathing hard. He looked

at the two girls malignantly, but he saw that
they were too tired to walk much unless he let
them rest, and, purely out of policy, and not at
all because he was sorry for them, and for the
hardships he had made them endure, he let them
sit still for a while. But finally he rose.

"Come," he said. "You've been loafing here
long enough. Get up now, and walk in front of
me—back, the way you came."

They groaned at the prospect of retracing
their footsteps once more, but he held the upper
hand, and there was nothing for it but obedience.
That much was plain. Desperately, as they began to drag their tired feet once more along the
trail, they listened, hoping against hope for the
sounds that would indicate that some of the
searchers they were sure filled the woods were
in the neighborhood.

But no comforting shouts greeted them. The
woods were silent, save for the calls of birds
and animals, which, friendly though they might
be, were powerless to aid the two girls against

this traditional enemy of every furred and feathered creature in the forest.

Steadily they plodded on. Bessie knew the ground well by this time, and, one by one they passed the landmarks she knew so well, until they came at last to the cross path which had brought Bessie back to the trap Lolla had prepared for her. And there they came upon a startling interruption of their journey.

For suddenly Lolla herself, who had evidently been hiding there when they had passed, alone, before their meeting with John, sprang out and stood in front of them. Long as she had resisted her fear of the supernatural force that had come to the aid of the girls, she was plainly afraid of it still, for at sight of them her cheeks paled, and she cried out in terror. And behind her, as scared as she was herself, came Peter, the big gypsy, shaking in every limb.

"A fine mess you made of things—letting them escape," growled John, as he saw his two compatriots. "If I hadn't found them on the trail, by sheer luck, they'd have been back at the lake by this time.''

"Let them go—for heaven's sake, let them go, John," wailed Lolla. "There is a devil fighting for them—he will kill you if you try any longer to keep them from their friends.''

"Pah! What child's talk is this? Be thankful that I do not beat you with my stick for letting them get free!''

"Listen to her, John," said Peter, warningly. "She speaks the truth. It was a devil that spoke from the air. I saw his horns and his red tail. Be careful—he may be here now.''

John laughed, scornfully.

"Run away, if you are afraid," he said. "I will manage alone now. I would not trust you—you have failed me once, both of you. Do not think you can frighten me into failure because you are as brave as a—chicken!''

"Let them go, I say," said Peter, with a sternness in his voice that gave Bessie a new ray of hope. "I have had my warning, I will profit by it.''

"You coward!" sneered John.

But that was too much for Peter. With a cry of rage he sprang forward.

"I fear no man, no man I can see or touch," he cried. "And no man shall call me coward!"

In a moment the two were grappling in a furious fight. John was smaller than Peter, but he was wiry and as lithe and powerful as a trained athlete, so that he was a match, at first, for the rugged strength of Peter. But he had had a hard day, and gradually Peter's strength wore him down, and, as they crashed to the ground together, Peter was on top, and plainly destined to be victor in the fight. He looked up at the two girls.

"Go!" he said. "I will have nothing to do with you. I am fighting with my friend to save him, not for your sakes, you who have a devil to help you. If he keeps you harm will come to him. John, listen to me: I do this because you are my friend."

Bessie and Dolly needed no second invitation.

Amazing as was this latest intervention in their favor, they were too happy to stop to question it. It was their chance to escape, and five minutes later they were out of sight, and making their way, as fast as their tired bodies would allow them to do, toward Long Lake and safety.

CHAPTER XIII

Indeed, any lingering fear Bessie and Dolly might have had that John had succeeded in escaping from his two anxious friends who were so determined to protect him against his own recklessness, was dissipated before they came in sight of the lake, when, at a crossing of the trail, a glad cry hailed them and a sturdy guide stepped across their path.

"Well, I'll be hornswoggled!" he exclaimed. "Ain't you the two that was lost, or stolen by that gypsy critter?"

"We certainly are," said Dolly and Bessie, in one breath. "Were you looking for us?"

"Lookin' fer you!" he exclaimed. "Every one in these here woods has been a-lookin' fer you two since sun-up, I guess. Godfrey. but we was scared! Didn't know but that there gypsy might have sneaked you clean out of the woods! How did you all ever come to get loose? Or was you just plain lost?"

"No, we weren't lost," said Bessie. "He carried Dolly off all right; this is Dolly Ransom, you know. But he didn't catch me."

"Then how in tarnation did you come to be lost, too? You was, wasn't you? They told us two girls was missin'."

"Well, we were asleep in the open air, outside the tent, and I woke up just as he was carrying Dolly off. I didn't wake up until he'd got out of the firelight, and there wasn't any use calling anyone else. So I just followed myself."

"She says anyone would have done it," Dolly broke in, her eyes shining. "But I don't believe it, do you?"

"No, by Godfrey!" he said, emphatically. "A greenhorn, goin' out in them woods at night, in the dark, and a girl, at that? I guess not!"

He looked at Bessie, as if puzzled to learn that she had actually done such a thing.

"Well, you're all right now," he said. "Here, I'll just give the signal we fixed up. Listen, now!"

He raised his rifle, and, pointing it straight in the air, fired two shots, and then, after a brief interval, two more.

"The sound of that'll carry a long way," he explained, "and that means that you're both found. The other fellows who are searchin' for you will quit lookin', now, and come into Long Lake. If I'd fired just two shots, and hadn't fired the second two, that would have meant that one of you was found, and they'd have kept right on a-lookin' fer the other. I'll walk along with you now, an' I guess that varmint won't bother you no more. If he does—"

He patted his rifle with a gesture that spoke more plainly than words could have done.

"Tell me all about it as we go along," he said. "I guess maybe there'll be some work for us to do after we all get together—runnin' those gypsies out. They're a bad lot, but this is the fust

time they ever done anythin' around here that
give us a real chance to get even with them.
We've suspected them of doin' lots of things, but
a deer can't tell you who killed him out o' season,
'specially when all you find of the deer is a little
skin and bones."

He listened admiringly as Bessie told her story.
At the tale of Lolla's treachery he laughed.

"They're all tarred with the same brush," he
said. "One's as bad as another."

And when he heard of the trick by which Dolly
had worked on the superstitious fears of Lolla
and Peter his merriment knew no bounds, and
he absolutely refused to keep on the trail until
Dolly had given him a demonstration of just
how she had managed it.

"Well, by Godfrey!" he said, when she had
thrown her voice far overhead, and once so that
it seemed to come from just above his shoulder.
"Don't that beat the Dutch! I don't wonder you
skeered 'em! You'd have had me goin', I guess,
an' I ain't no chicken, nor easy to skeer, neither.

You two certainly done a smart job gettin' away from them.''

And so, when they reached Long Lake, the girls and the guides, who had scattered all over the woods searching for them, agreed, when they straggled in, one party after another. Eleanor Mercer was one of the first to return, and when she had finished proving her gratitude for their safe return, she turned a laughing face toward the chief guide.

''Do you know the thing that pleases me best about this, Andrew?'' she asked him.

''I can guess, ma'am,'' he said, with a grin. ''You told us when you come up here that you was goin' to prove that a party of girls could get along without help from men. And I reckon it looked to you this morning as if you was goin' to need us pretty bad, didn't it?''

''It certainly did, Andrew,'' she answered, gravely. ''And I don't want you to think for a moment that we're not grateful to you for the way you turned out and scoured the woods.''

"Don't talk of gratitude, Miss Eleanor. We've known you for years, but even if we'd never seen you before, and didn't know nothin' about the girls that thief had stolen, we'd ha' turned out jest the same way to rescue them. An' I guess any white men anywhere would ha' done the same thing.

"But if it was only us you'd had to depend on, I'm afraid the young lady'd still be out there. It was her friend that saved her. Too bad she trusted that Lolla witch. If she'd gone to Jim Skelly when she was near the gypsy camp that time, an' told him where her chum was, he'd have had her free in two shakes of a lamb's tail."

"I think Dolly and Bessie must be awfully hungry," said Zara, who had listened with shining eyes to the tale of her friends' adventures.

"Oh, they must, indeed!" said Eleanor, remorsefully. "And here we've been listening to them, and letting them talk while they were starving."

She turned toward the fire, but already two of
the guides had leaped forward, and in a moment
the smell of crisp bacon filled the air, and coffee
was being made.

"Oh, how good that smells!" said Dolly. "I
am hungry, but it was so exciting, remembering
everything that happened, that I forgot all about
it! Isn't it funny? I was dreadfully scared when
I was alone there, and again afterward, when we
thought we were safe, and that horrid man caught
us.

"But now that it's all over, it seems like good
fun. If one only knew that everything was coming out all right when things like that happen,
one could enjoy them while they were going on,
couldn't one? But when one is frightened half to
death there isn't much chance to think of how
nice it's going to be when it's all over, and you're
safe at home again."

"That's just the trouble with adventures,
Dolly," said Eleanor. "You never can be sure
that they will come out all right, and lots of times

they don't. It's like the thrilling story that the man told about being chased by the bear.''

''What was that, Miss Eleanor?''

''Well, he told about how the bear chased him, and he got into a trap, and the bear was between him and the only way of getting out, and it seemed to him as if he was going to be killed. So they asked him what happened; how he got away?''

''And how did he?''

''He said he didn't; that the bear ate him up!''

''Miss Eleanor,'' said Andrew, the old chief guide, as the two girls began ravenously to eat the tempting camp meal that the other guides had so quickly prepared, ''we've got something more to do here.''

Eleanor looked at him questioningly.

''We've got to find that gypsy,'' he said, ''and see that he spends the night in jail, where he belongs. If I'm not mistaken, he'll spend a good many nights and days there, too, after he's been tried.''

"I suppose he must be caught and taken to a place where he can be tried," said Eleanor. "I don't like the idea of revenge, but—"

"But this ain't revenge, Miss Eleanor. If you was a-goin' to say that you was quite right. It's self protection, and protection for young girls everywhere."

"Yes, you're right, Andrew. Well, what do you want me to do? I am afraid I wouldn't be much good in helping you to catch him."

Andrew laughed heartily.

"I ain't sayin' that, ma'am, but there's men enough of us to catch him, all right. Maybe you didn't notice it, but I sent out some of the men 'most as soon as they got here, just so's they'd be able to fix things for him to have to stay where we could catch him. Trouble is, none of us don't know him when we see him. I was wonderin'—"

"Oh, no, not now, Andrew. I know what you mean. You want the girls to go with you, so as to point him out, don't you? But they're so

tired, I'm sure they couldn't do any more tramping today.''

"I know they're tired, ma'am, and I wasn't
aimin' to let them do any more walkin'. I've
got more sense than that. But we could rig
up a sort of a swing chair, so's two of the
boys could carry one of them, easily. Then we
could take her over there, and she could tell
us which was him, and never be tired at all.
She'd be jest as comfortable, ma'am, as if she
was a settin' here by the lake, watchin' the
water.''

"Well, I suppose we can manage it if you do
it that way, Andrew, if you think it's really necessary.''

When it came to a choice, since it was necessary for only one of the girls to go, Dolly insisted
on being the one.

"Bessie is much more tired than I am," she
said, stoutly. "I was carried a good part of the
way and she tramped all around with that
wretched little Lolla, when she thought Lolla

wanted to help her get me away. So I'm going, and Bessie shall stay here and rest.''

''Don't make no difference to me,'' said Andrew. ''Let the other girls come along with us, if you like, Miss Eleanor. And you can stay behind here with the one that stays to rest. See?''

And so it was arranged. Bessie, lying on a cot that had been brought from Eleanor's tent, watched Dolly being carried off in the litter that had been hastily improvised, and Eleanor sat beside her.

''You've certainly earned a rest, Bessie,'' said Eleanor, happily. It delighted her to think that Bessie, whom she had befriended, should prove herself so well worthy of her confidence. ''I don't know what we'd have done without you. I'm afraid that Dolly would still be there in the woods if you'd just called us, as most girls would have done.''

''I don't quite understand one thing, even yet, Bessie,'' continued Eleanor, frowning. ''You know, at first, it seemed as if the idea we had was

3—C14

right; that this man had some crazy idea that he might be able to make a gypsy of Dolly.

"I'm beginning to think that there was some powerful reason back of what he did; that he expected to make a great deal of money out of kidnapping her. It seems, too, as if he knew where we were going to be, and who we all were, more than he had had any chance to find out."

"I thought of that, too," said Bessie. "If it had been Zara he tried to steal—but it was Dolly. And she hasn't been mixed up at all in our affairs."

"I know, and that's what is so puzzling, Bessie. Maybe if they catch him, though, he'll tell why he did it. I think those guides will frighten him. They're all perfectly furious, and they'll make him sorry he ever tried to do anything of the sort, I think— Why, Bessie! What's the matter?"

"Don't turn around, Miss Eleanor. But I saw a pair of eyes, just behind you. I wonder if he could have sneaked back around and come here?"

"Oh, I wish we'd had one of the men stay. I was afraid of something like that, Bessie."

"I'm going to find out, Miss Eleanor. I'll pretend I don't suspect anything, and get up to go into the tent. Then, if it's John, I think he'll show himself."

She rose, and in a moment their fears were confirmed. John, his eyes triumphant, stepped out, abandoning the concealment of the bushes.

"Where is the other?" he said. "The one called Bessie—Bessie King? It's not you I want—"

"Hands up!" cried the voice of Andrew, the chief guide.

And the gypsy, wheeling with a savage cry, faced a half circle of grinning faces. He made one wild dash to escape, but it was useless, and in a moment he was on the ground, and his hands were tied. In the struggle a letter fell from his pocket, and Bessie picked it up. Suddenly, as she was looking at it idly, she saw something that made her cry out in surprise, and the next mo-

ment she and Miss Mercer were reading it together.

"Get this girl, Bessie King, and I will pay
you a thousand dollars," it read. "She is dark,
and goes around with a fair girl called Dolly. It
will be easy, and if you once get them to me and
out of the woods, I will pay you the money, and
see that you are not in danger of being arrested.
I will back you up."

"Who wrote that letter? Turn over, quickly!"
cried Eleanor.

"I know without looking," said Bessie. "Now
we can guess why he was so reckless; why he took
such chances! He thought I was Dolly, because
of that mistake about our hair! Yes, see; it is
Mr. Holmes who sent him this letter!"

CHAPTER XIV

But, despite the revelation of that letter, the gypsy himself maintained a sullen silence when efforts were made to make him tell all he knew and the reason for his determined effort to kidnap Dolly. He snarled at his captors when they asked him questions, and so enraged Andrew and the other guides by his refusal to answer that only Eleanor's intervention saved him from rough handling.

"No, I won't let you use violence, Andrew," said Eleanor, firmly. "It would do no good. He won't talk; that is his nature. You have him now, and the law will take him from you. There isn't any question of his guilt; there will be evidence enough to convict him anywhere, and he will go to prison, as he deserves to do. All I hope is that he won't be the only one, that we can get the

213

man who bribed him to do this, and see that he gets punished properly, too.''

''I'm sure with you there, ma'am,'' said old Andrew. ''He's a worthless critter enough, I know, but he ain't as bad as the man that set him on. If the law lets that other snake go, ma'am, jest you get him to come up here for a little hunting, and we'll make him sorry he ever went into such business. I'd like to get my hands on him. I'm an old man, but I reckon I'm strong enough to thrash any imitation of a man what would play such a cowardly trick as that. Afraid to do his own dirty work, is he? So he hires it done. Well, much good it's done him this time.''

''I'll keep this letter,'' said Eleanor. ''I think it was mighty foolish of him to sign his name to it. It's a pretty good piece of evidence against the man, if he is rich and powerful. If there's any justice to be had, I think he'll suffer this time.''

''How did you ever get back here, just when you were so badly needed?'' Bessie asked Andrew.

He smiled at that.

"Well, we get sort o' used to readin' tracks in our work around here, Miss, and we seen that someone who might be this feller was doublin' around mighty suspicious. So, bein' some worried about leavin' you two here alone anyhow, I decided to come back with three or four of the men here, an' we did it, leavin' the others to go on an' see if they could pick up the other two gypsies.

"To tell the truth, I thought it'd be mighty strange if we found him anywhere near that camp. Seemed like he must know that we'd be lookin' fer him, and that there was the fust place we'd go to. So here we were, and mighty timely, as you say, Miss."

It was no great while before the sounds of the other party, returning, resounded through the woods, and soon Lolla and Peter, the man bound, and the girl carefully guarded by two guides, each of whom held one of her arms, were brought into the clearing about the camp. Lolla, at the sight of John, lying against a tree, his arms and his feet bound, gave a cry of rage, and, snatching her arms from her guardians, ran toward him, wailing.

"Go away, you fool!" muttered John. "This is your doing. If you and Peter had not been afraid of your own shadow, this would not have happened. I am glad they have caught you; you will go to prison now, like me."

"Look here, young feller," said Andrew, angrily, "that ain't no way to talk to a lady, hear me? She may be a bad one, but she's stuck to you. If you get off any more talk like that I'll see if a dip in the lake will make you feel more polite like. See?"

John gave no answer, but relapsed into his sullen silence again.

Eleanor approached Lolla gently.

"We are not angry with you, Lolla," she said, kindly. "No, nor with John. You love him, do you?"

Lolla gave no answer, but looked up into

Eleanor's face with eyes that spoke plainly enough.

"I thought so. Then you do not want him to go to prison? Try to make him tell why he did this. If he will do that, perhaps he can go free, and you and Peter, too. You wouldn't like to have to leave your people, and not be able to travel along the road, and do all the things you are used to doing, would you?

"Well, I am afraid that is what will happen to you, unless John will tell all he knows. They will take you away, soon now, and you will go down to the town and there you will be locked up, all three of you, and you and John will not even see one another, for a long time—two or three years, maybe, or even longer—"

Still Lolla could not speak. But she began to cry, quietly, but with a display of suffering that moved Eleanor. After all, she felt Lolla was little more than a girl, and, though she had done wrong, very wrong, she had never had a proper chance to learn how to do what was right.

"I'm sorry for you, Lolla," said Eleanor. "We all are. We think you didn't know what you were doing, and how wicked it was. I will do my best for you, but your best chance is to make John tell all he knows."

"How can I? He blames me. He says if I and Peter hadn't been such cowards all would have been well. He is angry at me; he will not forgive me."

"Oh, yes, he will, Lolla. I am sure he loves you, and that he did this wicked thing because he wanted to have much money to spend buying nice things for you; pretty dresses, and a fine wagon, with good horses. So he will be sorry for speaking angrily to you, soon, and you will be able to make him tell the truth, if you only try. Will you try?"

"Yes," decided Lolla, suddenly. "I think you are good—that you forgive us. Do you?"

"I certainly do. After all, you see, Lolla, you haven't done us any harm."

Lolla pointed to Bessie.

"Will she forgive me?" she inquired. "I tricked her—made a fool of her—but she made a fool of me afterward. I lied to her; will she forgive me, too, like you?"

"Did you hear that, Bessie?" asked Eleanor, by way of answer to the gypsy girl's question.

"Yes," said Bessie. "I'm sorry you did it, Lolla, because I only wanted to help your man, and if you hadn't done what you said you were going to do, and helped me to get Dolly away from him, he wouldn't be in all this trouble now.

"But you didn't understand about that, and you helped your own people instead of a stranger. I don't think that's such a dreadful thing to do. It's something like a soldier in a war. He may think his country is wrong, but if there's a battle he has to fight for it, just the same."

"But remember that the best way to help John now is to make him see that he has been wrong, and to try to make him understand that he can make up for his wickedness by helping us to punish the bad man who got him to do this," said

Eleanor. "That man, you see, was too much of a coward to do his work himself, so he got your man to do it, knowing that if anyone was to be punished he would escape, and John would get into trouble.

"John doesn't owe anything to a man like that; he needn't think he's got to keep him out of trouble. The man wouldn't do it for him. He won't help him now. He'll pretend he doesn't know anything about this at all."

"I will try," promised Lolla. "But I think John is angry with me, and will not listen. But I will do my best."

And, after a little while, which the guides used to cook a meal, and to rest after their strenuous tramping in the effort to find the missing girls, Andrew told off half a dozen of them to make their way to the county seat, a dozen miles away, with the three gypsies.

"Just get them there and turn them over to the sheriff, boys," said the old guide. "He'll hold them safe until they've been tried, and we

won't have any call to worry about them no more.
But be careful while you're on your way down.
They're slippery customers, and as like as not to
try to run away from you and get to their own
people.''

"You leave that to me,'' said the guide who
was to be in charge of the party. ''If they get
away from us, Andrew, they'll be slicker than
anyone I ever heard tell of, anywhere. We won't
hurt them none, but they'll walk a chalk line,
right in front of us, or I'll know the reason why.''

"All right,'' said Andrew. ''Better be getting
started, then. Don't want to make it too late
when you get into town with them. Let the girl
rest once in a while; she looks purty tired to me.''

Bessie and Dolly and the other girls watched
the little procession start off on the trail, and
Bessie, for one, felt sorry for Lolla, who looked
utterly disconsolate and hopeless.

"We couldn't let them go free, I suppose,'' said
Eleanor, regretfully. ''But I do feel sorry for
that poor girl. I don't think she liked the idea

from the very first, but she couldn't help herself. She had to do what the men told her. Women don't rank very high among the gypsies; they have to do what the men tell them, and they're expected to do all the work and take all the hard knocks beside.''

"You're right; there's nothing else to do, ma'am," said old Andrew. "Well, guess the rest of us guides had better be gettin' back to work. Ain't nothin' else we can do fer you, is there, ma'am?''

"I don't think so. I don't suppose we need be afraid of the other gypsies, Andrew? Are they likely to try to get revenge for what has happened to their companions?''

"Pshaw! They'll be as quiet as lambs for a long time now. They was a breakin' up camp over there by Loon Pond when the boys come away last time. Truth is, I reckon they're madder at John and his pals for gettin' the whole camp into trouble than they are at us.

"You see, they know they needn't show their

noses around here fer a long time now; not until this here shindy's had a chance to blow over an' be forgotten. And there ain't many places where they've been as welcome as over to the pond.''

"I shouldn't think they'd be very popular here in the woods.''

"They ain't, ma'am; they ain't, fer a fact. More'n once we've tried to make the hotel folks chase them away, but they sort of tickled the summer boarders over there, and so the hotel folks made out as they weren't as bad as they were painted, and was entitled to a chance to make camp around there as long as they behaved themselves.''

"I suppose they never stole any stuff from the hotel?''

"That's jest it. They knew enough to keep on the right side of them people, you see, an' they did their poachin' in our woods. Any time they've been around it's always meant more work for us, and hard work, too.''

"Well, I should think that after this experience the people at the hotel would see that the gypsies aren't very good neighbors, after all.''

"That's what we're counting on, ma'am. Seems to me, from what I just happened to pick up, that there was some special reason, like, for this varmint to have acted that way today, or last night, maybe it was. Some feller in the city as was back of him.''

"There was, Andrew, I'm afraid; a man who ought to know better, and whom you wouldn't suspect of allowing such a dreadful thing to be done.''

Andrew shook his head wisely.

"It's hard to know what to wish,'' she said. "Sometimes a man is much worse when he comes out of prison than he was when he went in. It seems just to harden them, and make it impossible for them to get started on the right road again.''

"It's their fault for going wrong in the fust place,'' said the old guide, sternly. "That's what I say. I don't take any stock in these new fangled notions of makin' the jail pleasant for them as does wrong. Make 'em know they're goin' to have a hard time, an' they'll be less willin' to take chances of goin' wrong and bein' caught with the goods, like this feller here today. I bet you when he gets out of jail he'll be so scared of gettin' back that he'll be pretty nearly as good as a white man.''

''Of course, the main thing is to frighten any of the others from acting the same way,'' said Eleanor. ''I think the hotel will be sorry it let those gypsies stay around there. Because it's very sure that mothers who have children there will be nervous, and they'll go away to some place where they can feel their children are safe.

''Well, good-bye, Andrew. I'm glad you think it's safe now. I really would like to feel that we can get along by ourselves here, but, of course, I wouldn't let any pride stand in the way of safety, and if you thought it was better I'd ask you to leave one of the men here.''

8—C15

"No call for that, ma'am. You've shown you can get along all right. We didn't have nothin' to do with gettin' Miss Dolly away from that scamp today. It was her chum done that. Good-bye."

CHAPTER XV

Morning found both Dolly and Bessie refreshed, and, though the other girls asked them anxiously about themselves, neither seemed to feel any ill effects after the excitement of the previous day, with its series of surprising events. Dolly, at first, was a little chastened, and seemed wholly ready to stay quietly in camp. And, indeed, all the girls decided that it would be better, for the time at least, not to venture far into the woods.

"I think it's as safe as ever now, along the well-known trails that are used all the time," said Miss Eleanor, "but, after all, we don't know much about the gypsies. Some of them may be hanging around still, even if the main party of them has moved on, and we do know that they are a revengeful race; that when one of them is hurt, or

227

injured in any way, they are very likely not to
rest until the injury is avenged. They don't care
much whether they hurt the person who is guilty
or not; his relatives or his friends will satisfy
them equally well.''

''I'm perfectly willing to stay right here by the
lake,'' said Margery Burton, ''for one. It's as
nice here as it can possibly be anywhere else. I'd
like someone to go in swimming with me.''

''If it isn't too cold I will,'' cried Dolly, cheer-
fully.

And so, after the midday meal—two hours
afterward, too, for Eleanor Mercer was too wise
a Guardian to allow them to run any risk by going into the water before their food had been
thoroughly digested—bathing suits were brought
out, and Margery Burton, or Minnehaha, as the
one who had proposed the sport, was unanimously
elected a committee of one to try the water, and
see if it was warm enough for swimming.

''And no tricks, Margery!'' warned Dolly. ''I
know you, and if you found it was cold it would

be just like you to pretend it was fine so that we'd all get in and be as cold as you were yourself!''

"I'll be good! I promise," laughed Margery, and, without any preliminary hesitation on the water's edge, she walked to the end of the little dock that was used for the boats and plunged boldly in. She was a splendid swimmer, a fact that had once, when Bessie had first joined the Camp Fire, nearly cost her her life, for, seeing her upset, no one except Bessie had thought it necessary to jump in after her, and she had actually been slightly stunned, so that she had been unable to swim.

But this time there was no accident. She disappeared under the water with a beautiful forward dive, and plunged along for many feet before she rose to the surface, laughing, and shaking the water out of her eyes. Then, treading water, she called to the group on the dock.

"It's all right for everyone but Dolly, I think," she cried. "I'm afraid it would be too cold for her. I like it; I think it's great!"

"You can't fool me," said Dolly, and, without any more delay, she too plunged in. But she rose to the surface at once, gasping for breath, and looking about for Margery.

"Why, it's as cold as ice!" she exclaimed. "Ugh! I'm nearly frozen to death! Margery, why didn't you tell me it was so cold?"

"I did, stupid!" laughed Margery. "I said it was warm enough for me, but that I was afraid it would be too cold for you, didn't I?"

"I—I thought you were just fooling me; you knew I'd never let the others go in if I didn't!"

"It's not my fault if you wouldn't believe me. All I promised was to tell you whether it was cold or not! Come on, you girls! It *is* cold, but you won't mind it after you've been in for a minute!"

"Look out! Give me room for a dive!" cried Eleanor Mercer, suddenly appearing from her tent. "I know this water; I've been in it every year since I was a lot smaller than you. I'm afraid of it every year the first time I go in, but how I do love it afterward!"

And, running at full speed, she sped down to
the edge of the dock, leaped up and turned a
somersault, making a beautiful dive that filled the
girls who were still dry with envy. And a moment later they were all in, swimming happily,
and enjoying themselves immensely. All, that is,
except Zara, who could not swim.

"Oh, I wish I could dive like that, Miss
Eleanor!" exclaimed Bessie, who had been one
of the first to go into the water.

"Oh, that's nothing; you can learn easily,
Bessie. You swim better than any of us. Isn't
this water cold for you? I should think you
wouldn't be used to it. All the others have been
in pretty cold water before now."

"Oh, so have I! You see, around Hedgeville
we used to go into the regular swimming holes,
and they never get very warm. There's no beach,
you just go in off the bank, and most of the swimming holes have trees all around them so that
they're shady, and the sun doesn't strike them.
They're in the shade all the time, and that keeps

the water cold. This is warmer than that, ever
so much."

"I tell you what we'll do, girls; we'll fix up a
spring-board and have some lessons in real diving.
Wouldn't that be fun?"

"It certainly would! I'd love to be able to
do a backward dive!"

"Well, this is a good place to learn; no one
around to make you nervous, and good deep
water. It's sixteen or seventeen feet off that
dock, all the time, and that's deep enough for
almost any diving; for any that we're likely to
do, certainly."

Later they talked it over again, when they had
dried and resumed the clothes they wore about
the camp, and Eleanor Mercer, her enthusiasm
warming her cheeks, told them something they
had not heard even a hint of as yet.

"A friend of mine is scoutmaster of a troop
of Boy Scouts," she said. "And he has teased
me, sometimes, about our work. He says we just
imitate the Boy Scouts, and that we just pretend

we're camping out and doing all the things they do. Well, I told him that some time we'd have a contest with them, and show them; a regular field day. And, just for fun, we made up a sort of list of events."

"Oh, what were they?"

"Well, we planned to start in, all even, some morning, and make a regular trip, cook two meals, and come back. And on the way we were to divide into parties; there are three patrols in his troop, you know, and we could divide up the same way. The parties were to keep in touch with one another by smoke signals—they're made with blankets—and there was to be a fire-making contest, to see which could make fire quickest without matches. And, oh, lots of other things."

"That would be fine."

"Then I got reckless, I think. I said my girls could beat his boys in the water—that we could swim better—I meant more usefully, not just faster, in a race, because I think they'd beat us easily in just a plain race. And I'm afraid I boasted a little.''

"I bet you didn't; I bet we can do just as well as any old Boy Scouts!" exclaimed Dolly. "I wish we just had the chance, that's all."

"Well, you have," said Eleanor, with a smile. "That's what I'm trying to tell you, girls. Mr. Hastings is over at Third Lake right now with one patrol of his troop. He got there yesterday and the way I happened to hear about it was that he was on his way over yesterday morning—he got in ahead of the boys—to help us look for Dolly and Bessie, when they were found."

"Oh, that's fine! And shall we have that field day?"

"Later on, before we go home, yes. But he began teasing me again yesterday, and I told him we'd have a water carnival any time he wanted to bring his boys over. And he said they'd come Saturday."

"We'll have to get ready and show them what

we can do, then," said Margery Burton, with determination in her voice. "My brother's a Boy Scout, and I know just what they're like; they think we're just the same as all the other girls they know. I tell you what would be fun; to get up a baseball team."

"Maybe we'll try that later," said Eleanor. "But right now we want to be ready for Saturday. So I'll teach you everything I can. And I'm quite sure we can beat them in a life-saving drill; their three best against our three. We'd have you, Margery, and Bessie, and Dolly Ransom."

So it was agreed, and they all began to practice.

"I wish I could do something," said Zara, wistfully. "But I don't believe I could learn to swim before Saturday."

"You could learn to keep yourself afloat," said Margery. "But that wouldn't be much good, of course. You'd rather not go in at all, I suppose, unless you could really swim."

"I know what I could do, though," said Zara, suddenly, after she had watched Bessie go through the life saving drill. But she would not confide her idea to anyone but Miss Mercer, who looked more than doubtful when she heard it.

"I don't know, Zara," she said, "I'll see. It seems a little risky. But I'll think it over. It would be splendid, but, well, we'll see."

Speed swimming, pure racing, was barred when Saturday came. But with Scoutmaster Hastings and Miss Mercer as referees, and three summer visitors from the Loon Pond Hotel, who had no prejudice in favor of either side as judges, several contests were arranged that called for skill rather than strength.

"In this diving," Hastings explained to the judges, "what we want to figure on is the way they do it. If a dive is graceful, and the diver strikes the water true, going straight down, with arms and legs held close together, you give so many points for that. I'll make each dive first; that will serve as a model, you see."

Scoutmaster Hastings was not speaking in a boastful manner. He was a noted diver, and had won prizes and medals in many meets for his skill. And, when everything was arranged, he did all the standard dives from the spring-board at the end of the dock, and three members of each organization followed him.

Bessie had taken remarkably well to these new tricks, as she considered them. Her powers as a swimmer no one had questioned, but it was remarkable to see how quickly she had acquired the ability to dive well and gracefully. And, to the surprise and chagrin of the Boy Scouts, who had expected, as boys always do, when they are pitted against girls, to win so easily that they could afford to be magnanimous, and to abstain from gloating, the judges were unanimous in deciding that she had done better than any of the six competitors in all five of the standard dives in which Hastings showed the way.

As there were six competitors, the judges awarded six points for first place in each dive, five for second, four for third, three for fourth, two for fifth, and one for sixth place. And in two of the dives second place went to Margery Burton, while one of the Boy Scouts, Jack Perry, was second in the other four.

To the disgust of the other boys, Margery was placed third in the four dives in which Jack Perry beat her, and Dolly, a good, but not a really wonderful diver, was fifth in every one of the dives, beating at least one boy in each. So sixty-six points altogether went to the Camp Fire Girls, while the Boy Scouts, who had expected to finish one, two, three, had to be content with forty-eight, and were soundly beaten.

"That girl that was first is a wonder," said Hastings admiringly to Miss Mercer. "I take it all back, Eleanor. But I didn't think you'd have anyone as good as she is. Why, she's better than you are, and I always thought you were the nearest to a fish of any girl I ever saw in the water. She could win the woman's championship with a little more practice."

"Maybe you won't crow so much over us after this," said Eleanor, with a laugh.

"Not about the diving, certainly," said Hastings, generously. "But that's tricky, after all. The life saving is going to be different. There strength figures more. I really think my boys ought to give a handicap in that."

"Not a bit of it," said Eleanor. "Women have been taking handicaps from men too long. They've got so that they think they can't do anything as well as a man. This Camp Fire movement is going to show you that that's all over and done with."

"Well, we'll go through the tests first," said Hastings. "Then your girls will know what they've got to beat, anyhow."

The tests for life saving were to be conducted on a time basis. From a boat a certain distance out in the lake a boy or girl was to be thrown overboard, and, at the same moment, the competitor was to leap in after the one who represented the victim and take him or her to shore, the winners being those who did it in the shortest time. Again, as there were to be six competitors, the first place was to count six points, the second, five, and so on.

First, the boys went out and went through their exercise in fine style. Although the boy who played the part of victim could swim, he made no move to help himself, simply staying perfectly still and letting his "rescuer" take him in.

Then, when the three boys had finished, with only five seconds between the fastest and the slowest, Eleanor and Hastings rowed out with the three who represented the Camp Fire Girls, and, as "victim," Zara!

Zara had insisted.

"I really would be drowned if they didn't save me," she said, "so it will be a real test."

And, with that added spur, each of the three girls actually managed to beat the fastest time of the boys. Margery was first, Bessie was second, and Dolly third. Hastings, as soon as he discovered that Zara could not swim, was full of admiration.

"That's the nerviest thing I ever heard of," he said. "Of course they did better. But it's your 'victim' that deserves the credit. She's certainly plucky."

"So I really did help, didn't I?" said Zara. "My, I was scared at first. But then I knew the girls wouldn't let me go down, and, after the first time, it wasn't so bad."

"Well, you gave us a surprise, and a licking," said Scoutmaster Hastings. "But we'll be ready for you when we have that field day. How about some day next week?"

"Splendid," said Eleanor. "And we'll give you a chance to get even."